Murder In Keswick

A Sherlock Holmes Mystery

William Todd

Copyright 2018 by William Todd

All rights reserved. This book or any portion thereof may not be reproduced or used in any manner whatsoever without the express written permission of the publisher except for the use of brief quotations in a book review.

Printed in the United States of America

First printing, 2018

Print edition via Createspace

Ebook edition via Kindle Direct Publishing

I would like to thank my family and friends who are my biggest cheerleaders. They are a constant source of encouragement to me to be the best writer I can be and to never give up, no matter how hard it can be at times to put words to paper—and believe me, it can be very hard. I would also like to thank my new friend, Ray Greenhow, who I met online whilst researching Keswick, England for the story. Mr Greenhow's insights into the area and history, along with countless articles and photographs were instrumental in helping bring my story to life. There will be more about Ray at the end my story.

1

Sherlock Holmes was never fond of what he called my 'over-dramatization' of his methods, or my 'sensationalizing' of the facts surrounding a particular case when I put it to paper. As best I could, I would relay to the reader only what was relevant to both story and method to display Holmes' unique abilities in deduction and logic. If adjectives were ever needed or more descriptive language employed, it was usually done only sparingly and to make the story more palatable. There are certain cases, however, that manifest from time to time, so wholly unique that it is a near-impossible feat not to over-dramatize or sensationalize the facts because they are just that—*dramatic* and *sensational*. Customarily, it is these cases that are left out of my accounts of the great detective. There are a few, however, that I feel display the quintessential Holmes ability despite their—in his eyes—garish underpinnings. The following account is just such a case, which, after much debate, my friend has acquiesced to it being put before the public.

It was Wednesday, July 20th, 1898. The train clapped along rhythmically, and the sun shone in fits and starts into our compartment as we rushed along the wooded countryside. We were making good time to Cumbria for a well-deserved holiday in the Lake District after a particularly gruelling stretch for Holmes in London. For six weeks he managed a mere three hours of sleep a night and on a few nights none whatsoever, which would be the utter undoing of most. He unravelled four separate cases for Scotland Yard and one for the Crown—a particularly nasty affair having national implications that I may never get to set before my readers. At first, he resisted the suggestion of rest in the country, not sharing the bucolic allure but I, at last, broke through my friend's defenses and convinced him that some time away would rejuvenate him for whatever London's seedy underground had in store for him upon our return.

Agreeing to the rest did not mean, however, that Holmes looked forward to it. He stared morosely out the window at the passing landscape, having previously kept himself busy with a copy of the Times; however, it had run its course an hour into the journey.

He had been quiet for some time, so I tried to break him from his melancholic reverie. 'You know, Holmes, this will do you good,' said I. 'The fresh country air, the bright sunshine...It will be cathartic to both your mind and body to relax for a few days.'

My friend glanced at me from the corner of his eye but kept his sullen vigil of the countryside. 'Watson, you know as well as I do that my mind never relaxes, and my body does remarkably well at keeping up. Those slaves are surely used to their master by now.' He turned and looked upon me directly. 'Sloth is the murderer of many a good intellect, Watson, and I can ill-afford the demise of mine.'

'Honestly, Holmes, I never knew a person who could look upon a few days' rest as a detriment to one's intellect,' I remonstrated.

I returned my gaze out at the passing scenery, trying not to betray the fact that I knew the man had a point. I was aware this was a calculated risk on my part, for when his mind had no problems to solve, no cyphers to break, no data to analyse, no criminals to catch, Holmes would sometimes fall into a despair resulting in his use of cocaine or morphine for artificial stimulation. This was especially true during times of acute activity followed closely by periods of indolence, which I was currently forcing upon my friend. Yet, as a physician I also knew that Holmes ofttimes pushed himself beyond safe boundaries and needed time for compulsory convalescence before his overworked body made the permanent decision for him.

'I know the pace at which that mind of yours works,' I finally replied, engaging him once again, 'even if I do not know precisely *how* it works. You need not concern yourself with any possibility of inactivity. There will be plenty to do in the clean air of Cumbria that will keep you *safely* stimulated, body and soul.'

He immediately understood my meaning and gave me a knowing look. 'Would you consider grappling with Moriarty at Reichenbach or his brash sibling in Gloucester *safe* stimulation? I dare say an occasional injection would be much more harmless than most of my other sources of impetus. But you need not worry, Watson. At the moment, I am sufficiently satiated.'

'I am glad to hear it,' I continued. 'Nonetheless, to keep you on that track we can walk the fells, row the waters, take in the ample clean air, and, allowing for rain, for inside activities, I bought you *The Gases of the Atmosphere* by Ramsey. I have heard you mention his name more than once during your chemistry experiments. It is a nice volume that I am sure you could get through within the week.'

With a resigned air and a somewhat weak smile, my friend replied, 'All things considered, I believe I shall relish the book the most.'

'There is much to be missed if all you do is read instead of engaging Mother Nature firsthand; however, if you want to immerse yourself in the workings of the atmosphere between the covers of a book for the entire week, the choice is yours to make. At least there will be no telegrams from Lestrade or Mycroft and no criminals to track.'

Holmes grumbled reproachfully under his breath.

I slapped him on the knee. 'The blackguards will still be there when we return, I assure you.'

Around half-past three our train finally pulled into the station at Keswick. Looking out the compartment window as we slowed to a stop, Holmes' slouched features suddenly ameliorated at the sight on the platform. There seemed to be subdued energy which was growing by the second. Passengers waiting for the train and their well-wishers alike were busy talking amongst themselves with such looks upon their faces that ranged from astonishment to horror. And their demeanor was not lost on Sherlock Holmes. As a dog hearing a sound his master cannot, he sat up straight in his seat and focused his keen gaze out at the animated crowd on the platform. I could tell by the look that overtook him he deduced something was amiss.

Finally, he jumped from his seat, retrieved his valise and made his way to the compartment door. 'Come, Watson, let us see what the excitement is all about.'

'It is nothing, I am sure,' said I as I retrieved my belongings and was quickly at his heels. 'Probably an animal coming to its end under the tracks of the train. I am sure it was probably quite a shock to those who witnessed it.'

Holmes paid no attention to my offering, and we were soon off the train and amongst the boarding passengers. He approached a stout, older gentleman and queried, 'Excuse me, sir, but could you tell me what has made everyone on the platform so aroused? We have just exited the train and seeing the state of those here made me quite curious.'

The man's bushy grey eyebrows raised in astonishment. 'Well, you will hear it soon enough, especially if you are staying in town. No more than an hour ago, word got back that a man's decapitated body was just discovered along the road to Penrith.' The man paused for a reaction, to which Holmes offered none, then continued, 'But the more astonishing part is that it was Mr Darcy of Muirhouse!'

Holmes' aquiline features transformed, and the gears in his machine-like brain, having sat idle for several hours, thus begun to turn once again. 'Pray tell,' he said with a quick eagerness in his voice, 'is there any word where they are delivering the body?'

As the man began to walk toward the train to board, he said, 'Near as I can tell, the constabulary...possibly the town hall. A small place such as Keswick obviously doesn't have proper facilities for this type of tragedy.'

'Thank you,' Holmes replied.

I, at hearing all of this, sunk at the realization that there most certainly would not be any resting on this respite.

Holmes read my disgruntled countenance when he turned to me. He said, 'It was foolish to think evil had not yet stained this beautiful countryside. I dare say, Watson, that when it rears its ugly head out here, so far removed from more authoritative eyes, it may even thrive.'

I did not try and hide my disappointment, and I knew that it would be fruitless to try and convince him to leave this to the authorities, so with a sigh of resignation I asked, 'What is the plan of action then?'

'We shall check in to the King's Arms, find out where the constabulary is, and pay the local authorities a visit.'

I nodded solemnly and picked up my baggage.

Noticing the devastated look on my face, Holmes only blinked at me emotionlessly then turned on his heel. Making haste towards the station entrance, he said over his shoulder, 'come, come, now Watson. Did you not want me to relax on holiday? Well, what could be more relaxing than solving a murder?'

2

Within a few minutes' cab ride, we found ourselves at The King's Arms Hotel. It was a white-washed and black-trimmed coaching inn on Main Street in the middle of the hamlet. It gleamed proudly in the brightness of the day. We asked our ride to wait for us, as we would be returning to leave again shortly. We then retrieved our things and stood looking about, taking in the scenery for the first time since we stepped off the train; quaint shops selling trinkets and clothing, smiling people (who obviously had not yet been apprised of the gruesome discovery) milling about the streets, the beautifully rugged, brown and grey-tipped Skiddaw and Cat Bells off in the distance for walking and climbing, the high summer sun above.

'It is hard to believe that such a calamity could happen here,' I offered as I took it all in. 'It is quite a lovely little place.'

'Abel was no doubt thinking a similar thought before he was bludgeoned by Cain,' Holmes quipped. 'Come, let us check our things and be off to the police station.'

The hotel's interior was ample and cosy with high, dark-beamed ceilings and walls that, despite its age, had weathered time well. As we passed it, I pictured myself next to the fireplace in one of the plump, leather chairs reading some new journals I had brought along, which I now knew would never see the outside of my carry-all while in Keswick.

After checking in and having our things taken to our rooms, we were back outside. We asked the driver of the cab to take us to the constabulary and were on our way, once again. If the body had been taken elsewhere, we would soon find out. A five-minute jaunt through the streets of Keswick landed us at our destination.

When we arrived, a young, ginger-haired constable was quickly descending the steps of the station putting on his police helmet, tucking back some stray curly locks. He wore an expression that seemed an amalgam of agitation and worry.

Holmes waved at him as we crossed the street. 'Good afternoon, Constable.'

The man hastily shook our hands. 'Hello, gentlemen, I'm Constable Wickham. And *good* is certainly not an adjective that I would use today.'

'Yes, it has come to our attention that there has been some dreadful accident,' Holmes replied.

'Accident would *also* not be the proper word in this case. Say, you two wouldn't happen to have any information for me that could shed some light on this ghastly affair?'

'I'm afraid not,' Holmes replied. 'We had just stepped off the train, and this was the news that greeted us.'

The constable waved us off and began walking away. 'I apologise for my rudeness, but I have some difficult affairs ahead of me, and I do not have time for idle chit-chat.' He said.

Holmes smiled. 'That is why we are here, sir. I am Sherlock Holmes, and—'

'And Dr Watson,' he finished with a hardy smile, returning and shaking our hands once again with more vigor. 'I have read many of your accounts of Mr Holmes, Doctor, and I can only say that it is indeed Providence that has led you here today.'

Holmes replied with an over-dramatic wave of his hand, 'We would be remiss if we holidayed with a murderer on the loose.' As if waiting for my approval, he then glanced at me from the corner of his eye.

'Yes, we would be happy to assist in any way we can,' I finally and reluctantly interjected.

'Right. Then please follow me.'

He led us around the back of the building where a wagon was waiting. Three men had just removed a blanketed body and were carrying it up the steps. To the men, he said, 'I have had two tables put together in the back room. We shall put the poor man there until the coroner comes over from Workington. It may be a bit of a wait on such short notice. I am still anticipating word from Chief Constable Dunne up in Carlisle.'

I thought the young man, though possibly no more than mid-way through his twenties, held himself up very confidently under the circumstances; however, it was easy to see from how hard he worked at it that the demeanor he now wore was not his usual disposition.

Wickham motioned for us to follow the men and their bulky package up the stairs, which Holmes was happy to oblige. There was a keenness in his step and a sharpness in his eyes. He had the attitude of an excited terrier after a rat. I wanted to be angry that a holiday of relaxation was turning into a typical day in London, albeit with nicer scenery and sweeter air; however, telling Holmes to stay out of a situation like this would be tantamount to asking anyone else to cease breathing.

The men placed the body on the table, and Constable Wickham thanked them and asked them to leave.

'As you may not be aware,' he said to us when we were alone, 'Keswick is a small community, and this sort of thing never happens.'

'That is a statement which unfortunately can no longer be made,' Holmes offered back.

'And it was a statement that I was once proud to make. At any rate, if not for the two of you for assistance, this would have more than likely fallen entirely upon my shoulders as Chief Constable Dunne has committed most of our meagre resources for this area to the Appleby horse fair.'

'Why would he have to commit so many resources to a horse fair?' I asked.

'It is not so many as you may think in an area that rarely sees such crimes as this,' Wickham said unpretentiously. 'At this fair, though, thousands of Gypsies come from far and wide. If a crime is going to be committed, rest assured it will happen around fair time. It has been over for about three weeks now, but the build-up and dispersion of the vagrants take a few weeks on either side. You will find the woods for thirty miles around filled with the lot, and most available constables are used for monitoring the migration to make sure nothing unsavory happens.'

'There seems to be a glaring hole in their efforts for something as tragic as this to unfold on their watch,' said my friend.

'I should say so, Mr Holmes. The occasional missing chicken, or a pick-pocket, or a minor swindle of one sort or another is the most I have had to worry about when they pass through Keswick. Nothing as heinous as murder, and certainly nothing as utterly gruesome as a decapitation. I am not ashamed to say this is beyond my purview.'

Holmes gave the man a weak smile and said, 'And we shall endeavor to help in what little way we can to clear up this matter. Let us now inspect what is before us. Watson, your medical experience shall be invaluable, I would wager.'

I nodded. 'I shall offer what I can.'

Constable Wickham took a long breath as he eyed each of us as if to ready us for what was under the sheet. Then, he pulled it back.

The body was that of a large man. Fully intact, he would have been well over six feet, thick but not obese. He wore a loosely-fitted grey tweed suit with a blue Tattersall shirt. Dress wellingtons rounded out the ensemble.

The first question Holmes asked was probably the most obvious one. 'Are you certain that this is, in fact, the Mr Darcy we were told had met this terrible fate?'

Nodding to the corpse, Constable Wickham replied, 'I am sure of it. I saw him in these very clothes just yesterday afternoon when he entered the Royal Oak, a pub just a few streets away. And, as you can surmise, even without the head, he is, er, *was* a tall fellow. He always rather proudly boasted of a nearly six-and-a-half-foot frame. There are a rare few in the whole of the Lake District that could match him for size and the few that can come close are either absent from the area or too old to pass their bodies off as this one. I am quite certain this is indeed the man, Mr Robert Darcy.'

'Who was the unfortunate soul to discover the body?' Holmes asked as he began examining the trouser legs and the undersides of the boots with a determined eye, picking something from the treads and putting it in his frockcoat pocket.

'Mr Marlott,' replied the constable. 'He walks the three miles over to Threlkeld to visit his ailing sister a few times a week. He cannot swear one way or the other as to whether the body was there on his initial pass around half-past nine this morning for he was on the other side of the road. He found it on his return roughly an hour and a half ago.'

As Wickham was talking, Holmes scrutinized each of the dead man's hands, whipping around the body energetically. 'There is some scuffing of the left shirt sleeve and coat, barely noticeable, nothing on the right. He was left-handed.'

'That is correct, Mr Holmes. Again, Mr Darcy seemed to be singular in that regard, as well.'

Holmes did not pay attention to the affirmation. He continued nonplussed, 'No abrasions. Clean hands and fingernails. He did not fight off his attacker. Being a member of the landed gentry, his hands seem quite rough and calloused.' He looked up from the body and engaged the young constable. 'He did not shy away from manual labor?'

The constable shook his head. 'No more than others of his station. He had, however, become an avid rower in the past few months. I believe the story making the rounds was that he gained some weight over the winter, and the exercise was Mrs Darcy's idea, though I cannot attest to the accuracy of that statement. He has a small boat in which I would often see him, especially on sunny days, sleeves rolled up past his elbows, rowing vigorously out on

Derwentwater. His roughened hands no doubt came from handling the oars.'

'Judging by the looseness of the clothing, the rowing must have had the desired effect,' Holmes replied.

'It did. He seemed much more fit, and I must say a bit happier, too. He mentioned to me not more than a week past that he needed to have his clothes tailored but had been too busy with renovations of his home to worry about such things.'

'When would you say this new pastime of his commenced?' Holmes then asked.

'It is hard to say, really, as most of the people who call this area home spend time on the lakes. But for Mr Darcy, I would say his interest in being out on the water became keener back in April, as the winter winds declined, and he could row without fear of capsizing.'

As the two were conversing, I began my part and inspected the wound where the head once was. It was an extremely clean cut and I said as much.

'Very good, Watson,' Holmes replied. 'The head and body were separated in one swipe. That would suggest that either Mr Darcy was taken by surprise and had no time to react or was incapacitated and did not put up a struggle.'

He then gave me an expectant look, which suggested that there was something more he wished me to add, some clue he had noticed and hoped that I had too. My gaze in return must have relayed to him my ignorance of it (to my consternation, it was a look which I often wore in the midst of one of Holmes' revelatory moments). Instead of enlightening us, he only sighed heavily and moved on. 'He was not bound,' Holmes continued, examining the wrists.

'So that means he was unconscious,' Constable Wickham interjected. 'But without a head, we do not know whether he was bludgeoned into unconsciousness or possibly inebriated and was passed out.'

'Or even poisoned,' I then added, noticing that my voice had a bit more enthusiasm than I had anticipated. 'Examining the stomach contents could indicate whether he had been drinking before the deed was committed, but I daresay that without the head, the only thing we could say with certainty is that for whatever the reason, he did not put up any form of struggle before he was relieved of his pate.'

Holmes furrowed his brows across that great forehead and rubbed his chin contemplatively as he took in the body. He said, almost to himself, 'Yes, several distinct scenarios do come to mind.' Then, engaging me directly, he added, I think hoping that I would finally see what he was seeing, 'Is there anything else you can glean from the wound, Watson?'

I inspected the bone, muscle, and vasculature of the neck with a more determined eye, trying to employ my friend's methods and ascertain what had caught his eye that I was obviously missing. 'As I said, the cut is smooth, and there are no notches in the vertebrae, which would indicate an extremely sharp instrument with a long blade.' I then surmised, 'I have heard that the Japanese have such a sword as could take a head off with one swing.'

'You are correct, Watson,' said my friend. 'A Samurai sword. The steel is forged in a particular way as to make it susceptible to an extremely fine edge. However,' he added dryly, 'unless the constable is aware of any local collectors of Asian militaria, I do not think Mr Darcy met his death by a Japanese sword.'

'Axes and broadswords are about the only things around here that could separate a man from his head,' Wickham offered. 'They are common enough among townsfolk and gentry alike. I could see someone putting a nice, clean edge on one of those and using it.'

'Yes, the physics of a weighty piece of steel with a fine edge, such a Scottish Claymore or a double-edged axe, would do the job splendidly,' Holmes offered. 'A bit like a guillotine, if done correctly.'

'Then there is the problem of the blood, as well,' I continued, pointing at Mr Darcy's collar, still trying to put a finger on what Holmes was seeing that I was not. 'I should think that there would be more blood on the collar than there is. If the blow came while he was standing, much of the blood would have spurted and puddled around his collar before he fell.' I turned to Wickham. 'Was there a lot of blood where the body was found?'

'Hardly any,' was his reply.

'I would think then that Mr Darcy was killed elsewhere and dumped where he was found, which would indicate that the murderer had an accomplice.' I then turned to Holmes, thinking I had hit on it. 'It seems to me that, from a cursory examination of the body, he was lying at an incline with his head facing down-slope and not standing when the blow came, which would explain the lack of blood on the collar. It drained downslope instead of onto the collar. That is certainly a possibility. What do you say, Holmes?'

'I say for someone wanting so desperately some quiet time in the country, the vigor in which you are tossing theories about is astounding.' My friend then smiled at me in that way he does when he wishes to give me credit for my attempt at replicating his deductive prowess, but nonetheless relishes the opportunity to tell me I am wrong. 'So, what you are saying, Watson, is that the man was killed on a hill? You have successfully narrowed the crime scene down to ninety-percent of the surrounding countryside.' He then turned to the constable and said, 'Could you take us to where Mr Darcy was found?'

We procured a four-wheeler, and Constable Wickham took us to where the body was discovered. It was along the Keswick/Penrith road among a thick patch of oak and ash and pine that hop-scotched through the U-shaped valley. There was upon each side of the road a four-foot wide drainage ditch, and it was there that Wickham pointed as we descended our ride and crossed to the other side of the gravel road.

'This, gentlemen, is where Mr Darcy was discovered,' Wickham said as he pointed to a disturbed area of nettle and queen anne's lace matted to the ground. 'He was lying face-u...on his back, feet to our right and shoulders to our left.'

Holmes went down and scrutinized the area. As Wickham had said, there was little trace of blood amongst the vegetation. 'And what of our surroundings?' Holmes asked, looking up at us after a thorough inspection.

Wickham finally relieved himself of his helmet and wiped his glistening forehead with a hanky. 'About a half-mile back we passed the McGlinn's croft setting a bit back from the road. It's a little place that Morwenna and George McGlinn keep—a few sheep, which I think might have just recently been sold, some chickens, and a small plot of veg. The mister is a merchant seaman so he's not about much. Mrs McGlinn works in town at the Royal Oak to make ends meet when the mister cannot find work of his own.'

Wickham then pointed across the road at the open landscape beyond the wood. 'About a mile as the crow flies over those fells is the Castlerigg Stones, an ancient stone circle. They are beautiful yet disquieting in their barren setting, especially as the sun sets. The area around is dotted with walking trails that will take you to the circle. The stones are sometimes used in pagan rituals of one sort or another. Several times a year at night you can see their fires burning from a distance. The last fire was about the time of the Summer Solstice. Nothing like this has ever come from them, however. The worst we sometimes find are dead animals up there, which are promptly removed early the next morning before hikers begin to make their way.'

'And what of all the Gypsies you mentioned?' I asked. 'Is this road used in their departure from the fair?'

'This is one of the main thoroughfares in their exodus.' Pointing east down the road Wickham added, 'There is a campsite between here and Threlkeld, just off the road in the thicker woods. You can find a few families there. Several more beyond Threlkeld to Appleby, and a half-dozen or so west between Keswick and Workington.'

'And what of Mr Darcy's home, Muirhouse, I believe it is called?' asked Holmes. 'Where is its location?'

'A few hundred feet up from the shoreline of Derwentwater. Several walking trails from Castlerigg will take you right to the shores. It is roughly three miles south-west from here if I had to put a distance to it.'

As we all walked slowly back to the four-wheeler, Wickham asked, 'So what would you like our next move to be, Mr Holmes?'

As we all climbed back into the four-wheeler, Holmes' features darkened, and he said somberly, 'I believe it is time we inform Mrs Darcy that she is now a widow.'

3

We took the four-wheeler back to Keswick then followed a small road that Wickham told us circumnavigated the lake. Midway along the eastern side of Derwentwater, Muirhouse finally came into view as we broke through a tunnel of high-canopied trees. It was a beautiful country house built on the lower slopes of a lazy hill. The home was dressed in red sandstone that, along with its rows of mullioned windows, glistened in the late afternoon sun. It had crow-step gables at each end of its extensive length, and a bluey-grey slate roof with diminishing courses topped off the brilliant structure. A long, pebbled walkway just off the main entrance led three hundred feet or so to the lake shore and a rowboat lapping lazily against its small berth.

We were met at the front door by the butler before we had time to announce our arrival. He was an old gentleman with a dome of polished skin and a dark, thick blanket of side whiskers. His features relayed to us that we were too late. He motioned us inside. 'Mrs Darcy has been awaiting your arrival.'

Wickham grimaced. 'Mrs Dower?'

'She left not a quarter-hour ago, Mr Wickham.'

'Who is Mrs Dower?' I asked as we stepped beyond the threshold.

Wickham replied with irritation 'She is the bane of my existence. She's a nosy, old widow who thinks it her job to snoop and pry into other peoples' affairs and sets about fires of gossip, which I, in turn, must spend my time putting out. Once she heard about Mr Darcy, she, no doubt, spent all the energy in that tiny little body of hers getting over here to tell Mrs Darcy before any facts had been gathered.'

'Mrs Darcy is in the drawing room, gentlemen,' said the butler. 'This way.'

'Thank you, Alfred,' replied Wickham.

The home was exactly as a manor house should be. It was luxuriously appointed with ample accoutrements of plush velvet, gleaming tile, luminous porcelain, hanging crystal, and polished wood. The occasional stained-glass window added a splash of color from the bright, beautiful day beyond. Even an old suit of armour, hand raised for battle, added a cliched touch to the abode. Yet, there was a hominess to the décor that could not be ignored. All the rooms into which I could see appeared cosy and lived-in and not just set up to look like a sterile museum piece.

'The home is very nicely ornamented, I must say,' I commented as I looked around.

'You are right, Watson,' said Holmes. 'The womanly touch does a remarkable job of clothing the crumbling bones of this house.'

'Holmes!' I protested.

'No, he is quite correct,' said a forlorn female voice.

We all looked up to see the woman, Mrs Darcy, standing in the doorway of the last room on the right, just ahead. She was attractive even in her sorrow, and I wondered how much more so she would have been if the tears and sadness had been replaced with bright eyes and a smile. She was a tall woman with delicate, porcelain features, and her wavy, auburn hair was pulled back into a bun. She wore a bright blue summer dress, and in her hand, she held a well-used handkerchief.

'This was my husband's family home. It was in need of many repairs when we were married. We had just finished a makeover of the exterior and were planning renovations inside when...' She could not finish her sentence and just waved us in as she dabbed her eyes with the kerchief.

'I hope you don't mind, Mrs Darcy,' said the constable consolingly. 'I have brought along the great detective Sherlock Holmes and his colleague Dr Watson. They were just arriving for holiday from London when the...well, the news arrived. They are here to help.'

'I apologise,' she said to us, 'that your work seems to have followed you on your vacation.'

'It is a hazard of the profession, madam, and I console you on your loss,' replied Holmes.

She gave my friend a frail smile and nodded her thanks.

'You are American,' he noted as we took seats along a velvet settee on one side of a small mahogany table and a leather wing-back chair on the other.

'I am,' she said as she took her seat in the chair. 'My father was Ramsey Mitchell. He made his fortune in the oil fields of western Pennsylvania. We summered here once five years ago just before my father died. I met Robert, which sparked a friendship, correspondence, and, well…marriage.'

'I assume he knew about your wealth before the correspondence was struck?' asked Holmes, brow askew.

Her reddened cheeks widened into a smile. 'I know what you are implying, Mr Holmes.'

'I apologise, Mrs Darcy, but there does seem to be an influx of American dollars into the British aristocracy lately. I would be remiss if I did not ask.'

'And you would be correct, at least partially. I married Robert because I fell in love with him.' Her expression then slackened. 'He, on the other hand, married me for my money—at least at first. I believe he grew to love me as we spent more time together. At least that is what I hope. We never quarrelled. He was kind and generous. He was a gentle man despite his intimidating size. He did or said nothing that would convey to me the contrary. I tend to think women seem always to be the first to fall in love. They just need time to convince the man that he feels the same.'

There was an uncomfortable silence that followed, so Wickham then turned the conversation onto the matter at hand. 'As I am sure Mrs Dower has already apprised you, we discovered the body of your husband just outside Keswick on the road to Penrith. I am truly sorry.'

She nodded and began to wipe fresh tears from her eyes.

The constable became more apprehensive with what he needed to say next. 'Because of the...the way he was found we will not ask you to identify the body. That would not be proper. Perhaps we could get Alfred to do it. If his constitution is too weak, I am prepared to do it for you since I knew Mr Darcy well.'

She wept openly. 'Please, I could not ask anyone in the house to see him in that state. It would be too much to bear for any of us. If you...If you are certain it is him...' Her voice trailed off.

Wickham nodded slowly. 'I am. I wish to God I was not.'

I could see the growing agitation on Holmes' face, and I knew why. Inquiries needed to be made, as painful as they might have been, and Wickham was not inquiring.

So, Holmes did. 'Mrs Darcy, please forgive my impudence but when was the last time you saw your husband?'

I noticed Wickham's face redden in embarrassment, knowing he had neglected investigation for sympathy.

'It was yesterday, mid-morning. He was stopping over at the Royal Oak, as was his habit, for lunch, then he was catching the 1:30 p.m. train to Workington.'

'What was his business there?'

'That is where our contractor is located, as well as most of the supplies needed for the renovations. We had planned for a few months off from the work after the exterior was completed, but he was insistent that work get underway for the interior.' She smiled again as she spoke. 'I could see his eyes, as big and wide as a child's on Christmas Morning, as the splendour came back to the old place. I think he was anxious to see it to completion.'

'The name of the business with whom he was contracting?'

'Maubrey Brothers. Their offices are right next to the Hall Park Hotel in the town centre.'

By this time, Wickham had pulled out a pad and pencil and began writing down the pertinent information.

'And what was he wearing when you last saw him, top to bottom, please?'

'No hat, his tweed suit, and his brown leather brogues.'

The constable and I exchanged looks, but Holmes said nothing. He went on, 'Was he planning on returning or spending the night?'

'He usually spends the night as trying to catch the last train back to Keswick often has him cutting these meetings short, which he does not like to do. He is particular in what he wants and will go to great lengths to get it. No, I was not expecting him back until later this afternoon.'

'And he had an overnight bag with him?'

'He did.'

'We recovered nothing,' Wickham added. 'There was no bag when we found him. Was there anything valuable that he might have taken in that bag?'

Holmes sighed, which I think I may have been the only one who noticed. He did not like his train of thought interrupted.

'Not that I know of.' Mrs Darcy turned her attention to Alfred. 'You packed his overnight bag—was there anything in it anyone would have wanted?'

'No, mum,' said Alfred. 'Another change of clothes, his toiletries, and his wellies. That was it.'

I was not sure why Holmes was neglecting to bring up the fact that he was found wearing his boots, but I knew there must have been a reason. But I did wonder out loud—which only added to Holmes' consternation, 'Why would he need to take his boots when the weather has been so fine?'

The woman dabbed a tear at the corner of her eye and said, 'When you live up here long enough, Doctor, you realize that Mother Nature can change her mind several times in a day. One would be a fool to venture somewhere overnight without taking precautions.'

Holmes then regained the questioning, 'Why, Mrs Darcy, were you not a part of these meetings?'

'I am not a mousey wife, Mr Holmes, be sure of that. After all, it is my money which replenishes this home. This is Robert's ancestral home, and he knows how it should appear. I leave the structural renovations to him, and he leaves the interior decorating to me. It is a happy compromise. I do go to Workington often, both with and without my husband. I bank there, and there are several fine shops. Most around here tailor to the masses on holiday. I often spend a week or more in either Workington or Carlisle when I need a break from the solitude of Keswick.'

'And your last time there?'

'A week ago. I ordered new furniture for the library.'

'Did you spend the night, as well?'

'I did. As I said, the afternoon train comes back too early in the day to get anything done.'

'Back to your husband—tell me, did he always make a habit of mingling with the masses? Most people of his station would not stoop so low as to eat a meal at an inn.'

She pulled at her dress, trying to smooth out the creases. Mrs Darcy's voice held a note of pity when she replied, 'Robert did not come from money, Mr Holmes. This estate came to him only because he is the last of his family. The Darcy branch of the Muir tree had consumed their wealth long ago. He was part of several generations of the working class, so he feels—felt more at home eating chips and drinking ale than he did hosting a cotillion. That was the cruel irony—that he would get this crumbling, old house as a slap to his face of what the Darcy name used to be. He had two choices, Mr Holmes: either sit here and let the house fall down around him or find someone to help him renew the place and his name. When those big dark eyes looked upon me for the first time, I was only too happy to oblige.'

New streams of tears streaked down the woman's heartbroken face.

Holmes smiled and bowed his head. 'Thank you, Mrs Darcy. That should be enough for now. May we call on you should any other trifling questions arise?'

'If it will help catch whoever did this to poor Robert, you can call upon me day or night.'

Constable Wickham rose as he pulled out and examined his pocket watch. 'I apologise, but I need to return to the station as the coroner is due at any time, and I need to be there when he arrives. I shall return later and relay any more information if that is alright.'

'Of course,' Mrs Darcy sobbed.

Once we were back outside, Wickham turned to Holmes. 'I apologise Mr Holmes. You must think me an idiot for not posing those questions.'

Holmes waved him off. 'It is nothing, constable. It can be difficult sometimes to maneuver between being a friend and being an officer of the law. I am sure that you would have posed those very questions to Mrs Darcy...eventually.'

As we took one last look at Muirhouse before turning back down the gravel drive, I asked Holmes as I was still admiring its exquisiteness, 'How did you know that the house was in ill-repair? I saw nothing that would have given it away.'

'The stained ceiling from which hung that beautiful crystal, cracked walls hidden behind the oversized paintings, mouldy corners covered by French vases and suits of armour missing its armaments. It was all there, Watson. You did not see it because your eyes tend towards beauty—it is your way. Mine, to my benefit or detriment, tend towards what is beneath.'

'So, what is our next move?' asked Wickham as we turned onto the road that circled the lake.

'*Your* next move is to meet with the coroner,' replied Holmes dryly. 'Although I have a few things with which to occupy my thoughts with this affair, it is nearing dinner, and I am in need of some invigoration.'

'You do not wish to be present for the post-mortem?'

'I do not wish to step on the toes of authorities with whom there is a mutual unfamiliarity. You can be the liaison between us. I would like for you to do one more thing before you call it a day, however.'

'Anything Mr Holmes.'

'I think we already know the answer to it, but for clarity's sake find out if Mr Darcy ever made it on the 1:30 to Workington.'

'I had those very plans in mind for after the post-mortem.'

'Excellent. If there are any major developments between now and tomorrow morning, please do not hesitate to ring us up at the King's Arms. Otherwise, I would like it if you could breakfast with us in the morning and we can plan our next move.'

Wickham dropped us off in front of the hotel. As we watched him round the next block up, I asked, 'We aren't really eating dinner, are we?'

'You know me, Watson. My faculties become more acute when my body is not busy digesting food. Of course, *you* may eat,' he replied. 'But not here. The bright afternoon and pleasant breeze are perfect for a walk to get us acquainted with this little hamlet that is too comely for a murder. Let us take a walk to the Royal Oak.'

4

After a short walk, we found ourselves at the Royal Oak. It was a cosy, little coaching inn whose dinner service was already busy when we were seated. After ordering tea, I wanted to ask Holmes to relay what little clues had presented themselves thus far; however, I could tell by his knitted brow and direct gaze that his initial inquiries were not yet completed. He would, at these initial stages, rarely divulge any information. I believe it is an evolutionary adaptation on his part. For his species—the consulting detective—to survive, he must keep all his knowledge close to his vest until he is certain how all that data fits together, thus ensuring a proper outcome and the survival of a species of which he seemed to be the first. He would at times, though, indulge me. I was hoping that time would present itself shortly.

'Terrible tragedy, yes?' Holmes queried the robust and rosy-cheeked waitress when she brought our tea. 'We are here on holiday and just heard the news.'

She gave a nervous smile and nodded. 'Well, I hope that don't ruin your stay, sir. That sort of thing just don't happen 'round here,' she said. 'Especially to someone who was as well-liked as Mr Darcy.'

'Yes, everyone seems to have nothing but good to say about the man.'

Her face beamed when she said, 'He weren't like most folk with money. He weren't haughty or snobbish in the least. Why, he came in here to eat with regular folk all the time.'

'So I hear,' remarked Holmes. 'Tell me, how often would you say is *all the time*?'

She thought a moment then replied, 'Well, probably three days a week, anyway, always for dinner.'

'Was it always on the same days?'

'Heavens no. He was always out and about doing things, 'specially lately with fixing up his home down on Derwentwater. Never the same days but at least three days a week, I'd say.'

'Did you serve him his food?' Holmes then asked.

'No, Mr Darcy was a creature a habit and always sat at the same table. Morwenna usually served him.'

'Mrs McGlinn?'

'Why yes, Morwenna McGlinn. You know her?'

'No.'

'Then how'd you know her name?'

Ignoring the question, Holmes went on. 'Would she happen to be working presently?'

The woman looked around the room. Pointing, she said, 'That would be her, there.'

'Thank you, madam.' He reached into his pocket and pulled out a half-sovereign. 'This is for the tea. The rest is yours for your trouble.'

Holmes then rose from his chair with me quickly following suit. I could tell by the look upon the poor woman's face that she was unsure whether to be insulted at our abrupt departure or thankful for the generous tip.

We then reseated ourselves at a table in Mrs McGlinn's area.

'Holmes!' I objected quietly as we sat down. 'Do you not think that a rather rude thing to do?'

'I do not understand your concern, Watson. I paid for the tea and tipped her generously. It is what we would have done had we sat there the entire time.' He smiled as the woman approached our table. 'We are only here for a few days, and I do not have time to fish in an un-stocked pond.'

Morwenna McGlinn was a comely, young lady, petite in stature, with curly, flaxen hair and angular features which were starting to soften due to an obvious pregnancy. I would have guessed her to be in her second trimester. Her only blemish was a purplish bruise on her right wrist.

'Good afternoon, gentlemen,' she said with a bright smile and blue eyes that seemed to hold a prickly energy needed for such work.

Before she could offer another sentence, Holmes said with an exaggerated smile, 'Just a pot of coffee, please.'

'For you, perhaps,' said I, cutting in, 'But I would like something a bit more substantial. It has been a long day thus far, and I haven't eaten since breakfast.'

She gave me a wink and said, 'You look like a man who wishes to keep his physical attributes in check, so may

I presume, then, though you are hungry you do not wish to—*overindulge?*'

I am not ashamed to say that my cheeks became flushed at the question and was taken aback for a moment. After an awkward silence, I replied with a bit of embarrassment, 'Yes, just a little something to stay satiated.'

'Would a slice of venison pie do the trick?'

'That would be just fine,' said I.

'I will be back momentarily,' she said and off she went.

Holmes gave me a pathetic look and said, 'The gratuity for which Mrs McGlinn is working so diligently shall come from *your* purse.'

'Why coffee here when you initially asked for tea at our other table?' I asked.

Holmes eyed me lazily and quipped, 'It is not just a woman's prerogative to change her mind, Watson. Coffee invigorates the mind more than tea. I decided I need more stimulation at present.'

Mrs McGlinn returned to our table with our coffee and pie. As she was setting things down Holmes began, this time a bit more direct, 'My name is Sherlock Holmes, and this is my colleague Dr Watson. We just arrived on holiday and heard the terrible news regarding Mr Darcy. We are endeavouring to help Constable Wickham in this affair, and I was hoping you could indulge me a few questions, as I hear Mr Darcy was a frequent customer here.'

The young woman's eyes widened in surprise. '*The* Sherlock Holmes!'

'Are there others about?'

I resisted mightily the urge to kick my friend's shin under the table.

She waved off his cheeky response. 'Charlie must be thanking his lucky stars that you arrived when you did.'

'Charlie?' Holmes asked.

'Oh, sorry. Constable Wickham. We grew up together. He will always be Charlie to me, regardless of the uniform he wears.' Her features then curdled. 'It was a terrible thing what happened to Mr Darcy. I speak for all of us when I say we are happy that you are here to help, Mr. Holmes.'

'He frequented your establishment, and one of your colleagues mentioned you being his usual server. Do you mind if we ask a few questions, as this seems to be the last place Mr Darcy was seen alive?'

She put up a finger and said with an animated determination, 'Give me ten minutes, Mr Holmes, to settle accounts at my tables, and I shall be done for the day. You may then ask any question you like if it gets to the bottom of this ghastly tragedy. Mr Darcy was loved by one and all.'

'Obviously not *all*,' remarked Holmes matter-of-factly.

Mrs McGlinn was gone just long enough for me to finish my piece of venison pie and for Holmes to have two cups of coffee before she returned. She took a seat across from us, folded her hands together in front of her, sighed a weary sigh yet kept her smile, then said, 'Ask away, gentlemen.'

Holmes eyed her in that probing way for which he was known. 'We have previously established that Mr Darcy came in approximately three days a week for lunch. Is that a correct assessment?'

She thought a moment then nodded, 'Yes, that would be about right. There was a time in early May when he didn't come in at all for about three weeks, but I believe he was having to deal with some problems with a new roof. On a whole, I would say three days a week is correct.'

'And he always sat in the same spot?' Holmes continued as he then settled into his more introspective posture.

'Whenever he could. Sometimes, someone would already be at his table, but he would just set up nearby. He always liked being by the windows. The chill can sometimes be quite raw in these parts but sitting by the window with the sun beating through was a nice warming.'

'And can you recall what Mr Darcy usually had to eat when he lunched?'

'Oh, that's an easy one,' she returned. 'He gets the same thing every time he comes in. A piece of venison pie, which I am sure the good doctor can attest is rather tasty,' she said with a smile and wink in my direction, 'two pints of ale, never one, never three, and a few beet pickled eggs, which are a house favourite. That was it. Every time. He did not have the palate of the more stodgy gentry. He would eat, maybe strike up a conversation with a nearby patron as he finished his ale and be on his way.'

'And he followed this same procedure yesterday?' Holmes then asked. 'Same table, same food?'

The little woman's brow wrinkled. 'Of course. I served him myself. He sat at that table.' She pointed to a small, two-seat table half-way down the wall in the middle of a queue of windows. 'He came in around noon, ate his usual, and left about an hour later. He mentioned going to Workington for a meeting with a contractor about more house renovations.'

'And he talked to no one while here?'

'No one but me, Mr Holmes, and even that was very little. He seemed preoccupied, just stared off and had a long look about him. I can only assume it was due to that meeting he mentioned.' She smiled, winked (which she always seemed wont to do) and added, 'Maybe he and the missus had a row about the wallpaper and he lost. I have been told that she can be quite...resolute in her demeanour.' Mrs McGlinn shrugged her shoulders. 'Whatever the reason for his pensive disposition, after a bit, he paid his bill and left. That was the last he was seen till, well...' Her voice trailed off.

'Do you remember his attire?'

She thought for a moment. 'Just a tweed suit and an overnight bag.'

'Do you recall his footwear?'

'Brown shoes, I believe.'

Sherlock Holmes, who had thus been in a relaxed and meditative posture sipping his coffee, straightened his wiry frame. With an air of satisfaction, he said, 'Thank you, Mrs McGlinn. You have been most helpful.'

She looked at both of us with surprise upon her face. 'Really? I did not think I gave anything at all in the way of revelation.'

He smiled confidently at her. 'You would be surprised what can be gleaned from the most mundane information.'

She returned a grin and rolled back her shoulders in satisfaction. 'Well, I am glad that I was able to help in what little way I could, Mr Holmes. I only hope there was something there that could be of use.'

'There is one more question I would like to pose.'

She waited expectantly.

'What happened to your wrist? That is a rather nasty bruise.'

She lifted it up twirling it in the air in a manner of showing it was fine. 'It looks worse than it is, Mr Holmes. I have found that pregnancy and easy bruising seem to go hand in hand. I tried to slip through the door into the kitchen before it closed on me. With my size, I can slip through most things, but this time my wrist was caught between the door and the jam. Didn't hurt, hardly felt a thing, really, but I have this lovely bruise to show for it.'

I said, 'As a physician, I see that problem often. Green, leafy vegetables and citrus will help.'

With joviality she then added, 'If I had more money, I would go out and buy a dress that would match its color.

However, I suspect eating more cabbage is more within my means.'

Holmes nodded, and we rose from the table. 'May we call upon you again if the need should arise?'

'You can always find me here or at my cottage just outside of town, and I would be happy to help however I can.'

'Yes, I believe Constable Wickham pointed you out to us when we were examining where Mr Darcy was found.'

I looked around the crowded place then queried, 'Will you need an escort home, or will your husband be here shortly to retrieve you?'

She gave a hearty chuckle. 'Thank you, but I do not require an escort, Dr Watson. There is plenty of light left in the day and in less than an hour, I shall be resting my feet. With a husband who is rarely home, I have learned to be a very self-sufficient woman.'

'No one should be walking about by themselves,' said I. 'Are you sure you would not like some company for your trek home?'

'I am sure no one will try anything in the light of day, so my walk home should be uneventful if your worry is that I might end up like Mr Darcy. And for the darker hours, I have a hunting rifle and a dog for my protection.' She then rubbed her small but rounded belly, 'As far as my husband is concerned, he is a merchant seaman and is currently two days at sea on a ship bound for Tortola in the Caribbean. He'd been having a hard time of late finding a boat, but a week in Workington making his rounds at the docks finally paid off. And his employment could not have happened at a better time with our first on the way. If all goes as planned, before autumn arrives, he will have wired enough money back that I will be spending the rest of the pregnancy in the better climate of Cornwall with relatives, and he will join me there when he returns.'

'You will not be staying in Keswick?' Holmes asked.

'No, Mr Holmes. I have had about all I can stand of Keswick. She is a pretty place to visit during the summer but...' She sighed. 'And now with this murder. No, I will raise my child in a safer place with a bit more sun.'

I asked, 'How much do we owe for the coffee and pie?'

'On the house, gentlemen, courtesy of Mr Bruce, the owner. You have some admirers in this part of the country.' She gave us her customary wink, turned and skittered away, disappearing back into the kitchen.

'Well, she's a spritely little thing,' said I as we roused ourselves to leave.

'You still owe her that tip'.

On the walk back to the hotel, I finally asked, 'So what have you gathered from this grisly affair, thus far?'

'A few things, Watson. There is some light being shed, but the candle I hold is not yet strong enough to illuminate the room in which find ourselves. I yet need answers to some pressing questions.'

'Such as?'

'We shall start with the less obvious questions—why was he found wearing wellingtons when he left with shoes upon his feet? Judging by the hardness of the ground, it has not rained in well over a week, possibly two, which is rare indeed. If he was staying in town, meeting in town, and in a train for the journey there and back, what need would he have had with boots?'

He then produced a piece of vegetation from his pocket. 'I found this lodged in the tread.' It looked to be the trampled remains of a small flower with one remaining macerated blue petal. He continued as I examined it, 'I saw no such flowers on either side of the road, but I did see patches of blue higher up the hillsides all around. I surmise that his trek took him to the higher slopes where the earth is softer with the nightly dew. But why?'

'And why was his body found in the opposite direction of his travel? Workington is west of Keswick on the coast yet his body is discovered east of town? All interesting little trifles in and of themselves but answering them will be tantamount to the solving of this murder.'

I added, 'And the biggest why, to me, would be why decapitation? That is such a barbaric form of death.'

'Ah, yes, Watson, that is true, but the method of murder will tell you much. For example, was it because a bullet would have been too loud, and the murderer would have been found out? Stabbing may have produced the same effect. Crying out in pain, though not as loud as gunfire, might have still drawn unwanted attention.'

'So, you believe he was murdered in a place where his cries might have been heard,' I replied.

'I gave that as an example,' Holmes said, raising a long finger to emphasise the point. 'That is one possibility, but I did not say that is what I believe. Only more data will prove or disprove that theory. Decapitation also suggests a personal vendetta. The murderer wanted to see the fear in Mr Darcy's eyes before the act was committed. A bullet would have been too impersonal.'

He then shot me a look from the corner of his eye and said cryptically, 'Then there is the body itself. It did not tell me much, but what it did say spoke volumes, some of which I am not yet ready to articulate.'

'Well, what can you divulge at present?' I asked as we passed the intersection of Lake Road and Main Street.

Holmes sighed. There are times when he revels in knowing what others do not or cannot ascertain from their own observations. It is always the ace in his hand, and the man never tires of winning a game. Yet there are also times, I believe, that the great detective enervates of always having to lead people to facts that are, to him, as plain as the nose on one's face.

'I was hoping, Watson,' he finally said trying to hold back his exasperation, 'that while observing the intricacies of the decapitation you would have noticed something else.'

'I thought I had deduced all I could from it.'

'Did you not notice the angle from which the blade came?'

I thought back. 'It was a clean cut. Straight across the neck. What did I miss?'

Holmes' eyes brightened, and he smiled as he slapped me on the back. 'That was precisely what I was looking for!'

He could tell I was still in the dark as to his meaning, so he finally elaborated. 'The cut, Watson, was *straight* across his neck. If he were standing when the blow came, which I believe he was, and given his size, with a presumably smaller person wielding the instrument of death, the slice would have been at an angle, lower at the point of impact then rising. So, what would that tell you?'

I thought for a moment then postulated, 'He was kneeling or prone when the death-blow came. But I already deduced that from the lack of blood on his collar.'

'That is not the only possibility, Watson. Again, you make the mistake of not considering all possibilities once you have hit upon one. You must cast a wider net. If he were kneeling or prone why were his clothes not soiled or dirty, especially at the knees, if kneeling when the deed was done?'

'If it had happened on a clean floor there would be no need for stained or dirty clothes.'

'I can disprove both of your theories with three words: *The, blade, angle.* It tells a story, Watson, which you seem unable to decipher.'

'Please, enlighten me,' I replied a bit wounded at his veiled sarcasm.

'This time of year, it is a rare sight indeed for a floor to devoid of all dirt with the comings and goings of fair weather folly. Your hypotheses of kneeling or in the prone position were the first theories I discredited when I examined the body. For kneeling, there would have been indentations in the crease of his trousers at the very least. There were none. I say also, there would have been dust, dirt, crumbs, something on them and I found nothing. However, those trifles only corroborated what the wound had already told me.'

'Which was?'

'That Mr Darcy was standing when the blow came. You see, Watson, even if kneeling, the cut still would not have been a straight one. There still would have been an angle because now, instead of Mr Darcy being taller than his attacker, the attacker would now be taller than Mr Darcy. That is, of course, unless you want to postulate that the attacker was less than five feet tall.'

Rubbing my chin contemplatively, I remarked, 'Alright, Holmes, I see your point there, but what about prone? Why could he not have been lying on the ground when he was struck?'

'Because if he were prone, the tip of the blade would have hit the surface upon which he was lying, thus preventing the blade from cutting through that sizable neck of his. Therefore, it would not have been a clean cut. The murderer would have had to take several swipes to get completely through. Have I explained it sufficiently?'

I nodded acquiescence. 'It might take a bit to catch up to you, Holmes, but rest assured I do get there eventually. So, what other possibility am I missing?'

Holmes smiled as he opened the door to the King's Arms and let me through. 'There are two possibilities before us, Watson, one of which you had already hit upon earlier. Either the murderer was standing on something to elevate their height—'

'Like being uphill from Mr Darcy,' I cut in.

'Yes,' he said slowly to show his aggravation at my interruption. 'That is one possibility but not the only. Wider net, Watson. Wider net.'

'And the other?'

'The murderer was as tall as Mr Darcy. Deciphering which of those scenarios is the correct one will go a long way in putting this affair to an end.'

5

I left Holmes sitting cross-legged on his bed with his pipe and shag tobacco at his side and spent the rest of that first evening switching between reading a somewhat boring article on Sart sores and peering out my room's window, the latter quickly overtaking the former for being the more enjoyable endeavour. I had a wonderful view of Derwentwater in the foreground and the Cat Bells above it in the background. A nice breeze blew upon my face, bringing with it the comforting smells of the countryside, which relaxed me considerably. The lake itself was partially obstructed on my left by the roofs of other buildings, but I could see a large island in the foreground with a manor house partially hidden among its trees and a few smaller islands out in the distance, one of which at some time in the ancient past had housed a monk, Saint Herbert, I believe was his name.

After a final attempt at reading about sores failed, I retrieved my binoculars from my luggage, sat at the open window, and watched tourist and native alike as the sun inched ever closer to the hilltops. A few were in boats still out on the calm lake and some were strolling about the lake's shoreline close to town. But news of the murder must have finally seeped into their collective ear for the number of people out on such a lovely night was small compared to the crowds earlier in the day.

I aimed my binoculars through a clump of treetops on the eastern side of the lake, and I could just make out some lights at Muirhouse, which was partially obscured by the bell tower of a church. I wondered how poor Mrs Darcy was faring.

I finally retired at eleven and dreamt of being chased by a headless body.

· · · · ·

I was startled awake at 2:00 a.m. by knocking at my door. It was soft but insistent. As I rubbed my eyes awake, I could hear the harsh whisper, 'Watson. Watson!'

I put on my robe and opened the door. I saw through groggy eyes Holmes standing in the doorway with Wickham at his back. 'Come, Watson, and dress quickly. The game is afoot.'

'What in blazes are you talking about, Holmes? It's the middle of the night,' I said as I struggled with my trousers.

'Crime never sleeps, even in sleepy little towns. Young Constable Wickham has come to retrieve us. It seems Mrs Darcy has been burgled. Or at least there has been an attempt.'

Once dressed, we took a dog cart out to Muirhouse. We found Mrs Darcy sitting in the library with anxiety wrenching her features, clothed in only her nightgown and blue, silk robe. The manservant, Alfred, stood nearby awaiting any orders she might have. The french doors, which led out to a small patio overlooking the lake, were ajar.

Holmes sat across from her. 'Please tell me all that has happened and leave out nothing.'

She replied with some trepidation, 'Well, Mr Holmes, as one would expect, I did not wish to be bothered after hearing the news of my husband. In fact, it made me quite ill, so I retired early to my bedroom with orders not to be disturbed. Although I had cried myself to sleep, I did not sleep soundly. After some lengthy amount of tossing in my bed with the horrible thoughts of how Robert met his demise fluttering about my brain, I decided to get up and get a glass of brandy to help get me back to sleep.'

'Pray tell,' Holmes asked, 'where do you keep your brandy?'

'At present, it is in the drawing room. Alfred kept it close at hand for me all afternoon, and I had a glass earlier in the day to calm my nerves. I came downstairs to fetch another glass, and a moving shadow near the library startled me.' Here her brows knitted determinedly, and her voice became cold. 'Because of what happened to my husband, I did not take chances of the same fate befalling me, so I had a Derringer in my robe pocket. I said nothing and acted as though I had not seen the shadowed stranger, but if he was still in the library I was going to introduce him to the business end of my pistol.'

'That was quite a risk—,' I started.

'For a woman?' she finished, directing a steely gaze at me. 'One thing I am not, Dr Watson, is timid.'

'Duly noted,' said I, shrinking back just a bit.

She continued. 'I crept to the library door and peeked around the corner, but the intruder had slunk back out the French doors.'

Holmes then stood, crossed the room, and inspected the latch on the doors. 'Were these doors unlocked?' he asked as he pulled his magnifying glass from his pocket and scrutinized the door and lock.

Alfred seemed offended by the question. 'Absolutely not, sir! I personally lock every door in this house before retiring for the evening. I would wager my life that this door was indeed locked before I went to my room.'

Holmes then looked to Mrs Darcy. 'Did your husband have a set of keys for the house?'

'He did, yes.'

'Did he have them on his person when he left for Workington?'

'I do not think those keys ever left him.'

Constable Wickham spoke up. 'We took inventory of his belongings for evidence, and there were no keys found on him, Mr Holmes. In fact, there was nothing whatsoever found on him other than the clothes he was wearing.'

Holmes then asked the woman as he took his seat once more, 'Are you certain that the intruder was unaware you knew of their presence?'

Mrs Darcy shrugged as she replied, 'I did not call out, I made no sound whatever. The only thing I did was put my hand in the pocket of my robe to grasp my pistol and continued down the stairs.' She then added coldly, almost emotionlessly. 'I did not want the scoundrel to run. I wanted to confront him, for who would be trying to burgle the house of a man freshly murdered than the murderer himself? I was ready, Mr Holmes, for my pound of flesh.'

The only thing I could think was that this was certainly not a woman to cross. She had managed to replace entirely the sorrow for her lost love with a vengeful anger that did not mingle well with her otherwise attractive features.

'You have done well with your little feign, Mrs Darcy,' said Holmes with a hint of admiration. 'If the intruder thinks he was not seen, it might give him the courage to try again, and that is precisely what we want.'

Mrs Darcy added with a bit of remorse and a softening of her features, 'I even waited for fifteen minutes before waking Alfred to retrieve Mr Wickham. I had debated that same thought about him returning, then decided I needed more level heads to prevail in this matter. I am too eager to exact revenge on my husband's death, and I fear that anger may, in the end, take the wrong life.'

Constable Wickham asked, 'Do you think he was here to burgle or something more nefarious, begging your pardon, ma'am.'

'You mean was he here to exact on me the same fate as my husband? No, I think he had more material motives.'

'There is something here worth killing a man over?' Wickham then asked.

Her sigh was a long and laboured one. 'Something worth taking his head off for.'

We all stared at her in anticipation of her next words.

'I hadn't thought of it earlier,' she said. 'I was too distraught. However, after the shedding of some tears came a sobering clarity. Please, follow me.' She retrieved a small candelabra from the lampstand, and we followed her down the hallway past the drawing room, towards the dining hall.

As we were walking and passed the grand staircase, Holmes, asked, 'Where were you on the stairs when you saw the intruder?'

'I was about three steps down when I saw the movement. I did not have light. I know my way around well enough not to need one, so we were both but shadows to each other.'

'And he was heading in the same direction we are now?'

'I am not certain. He had only taken a few steps beyond the library doorway before the encounter, but I believe he was headed in this general direction.'

She slowed and stopped at the last door on the right. 'Here we are, gentlemen. The billiard room.' She lit the room by means of an electric chandelier, using a switch plate on the left wall near the doorway, which bathed the room in a harsh yellow light. As she did so, Mrs Darcy offered, 'This is the first room to get electric light. Robert insisted this room be wired as soon as we were connected, as he is an avid billiard player. The other rooms were to follow suit as part of the interior restoration.'

It was a large, rectangular room with plush red carpeting and darkly-panelled walls that was eerily reminiscent of one of the billiard rooms in a gentlemen's club I belonged to early in my practice. There was one large, uncurtained window that faced the back of the manor with a plaster bust, of some distant relative no doubt, centred in front. The woman walked beyond the billiard table to a rather elaborate painting of the Battle of Trafalgar hanging on the far-right wall and swung it to the left, revealing a large wall safe.

'If the murderous letch has my husband's house keys, he may also know about this.' She pulled from around her neck a long, gold chain attached to which was a small, metal key. She used it to unlock, then open the safe. Even from a distance, it was easy to see the bundles of currency stored within. 'There is always about eight to ten thousand pounds in cash in this safe to settle estate bills and just to keep on hand. I go to our bank in Workington once a month to replenish what we use. I was so devastated by the news earlier that this never even crossed my mind.'

'Apologies for my directness, Mrs Darcy, but how much are you worth?' asked Holmes.

'Not as much in pounds than in dollars', she replied phlegmatically. 'A little south of a two-hundred thousand, I think.'

The constable and I both gave a wide-eyed reaction to the revelation, but Holmes was unmoved. 'Even so,' he remarked, 'that seems to be a quite sizeable amount to keep in a home safe. You do not trust the banks with your wealth?'

'Not entirely, no,' she said. 'My father lost a fair sum of money he'd had in banks due to robbery—from within and without. In the early days of oil, western Pennsylvania was not the safest of places for money or life. I have not had the misfortune he had, but I am my father's daughter. I feel safer keeping a sizeable amount of my wealth close at hand just as he did. The rest is spread between three different banks—one in Workington and two in Carlisle...just in case.'

'And your husband had a similar key around his neck to access this money?'

'Yes, and we did not take them off. Ever.'

'I think we now know why your husband met his fate the way he did,' Constable Wickham said grimly. 'No key on a chain was found.'

'I feel like a fool for not seeing this earlier,' she said, her eyes welling with fresh tears. 'To think, the thing that had brought us together is the same that has taken him from me! And all because I am too afraid to keep it all in a bank.'

'Did anyone outside the walls of this house know about this safe?' Holmes queried.

Dabbing her eyes on the sleeve of her robe, Mrs Darcy said, 'To my knowledge, no one outside this home knew or needed to know, frankly.'

'Well, I dare say the secret is out now,' quipped Wickham.

I asked, 'Why did he not come through the window in here? He would not have had to skulk about in the shadows and risk being found out.'

'He might have tried,' Mrs Darcy countered, 'but that window sill is warped and has been long painted shut to help keep out the damp draughts. The window replacements at the back of the house are a bit behind. The wife of the contractor we employed to do the job has fallen ill so he is behind while he helps his wife recover.'

'I am afraid, Mrs Darcy,' Holmes then proffered, 'that this means you are no longer safe here. Is there somewhere you can stay for a few days? Friends, relatives?'

'No relatives. Robert is the last of his family. He had hopes of fixing up the estate and me giving him an heir to pass it on to. I can stay in town at one of the hotels.'

'No,' Holmes replied. 'I have an idea, but for it to work you need to be seen leaving Keswick.'

'I do have a friend in Carlisle, Emilia Rutherford. She is the daughter of one of my bankers. I can make arrangements in the morning to visit her for a few days, but

I do not like leaving my home open and empty for thieves and murderers to plunder while I am gone.'

With a glint in his eyes and the tiniest of grins, Holmes, replied, 'Trust me, madam, that is precisely what we want. The home will be open, but it most assuredly will not be empty.'

6

We—Holmes, Wickham, and I—spend the rest of the night in the library, keeping vigil, to make sure the intruder did not return. Sore and tired, we all left Muirhouse at a little before 6:00 a.m. to nap—if that were even possible—change clothing, toilet, and meet back at the King's Arms for breakfast at eight. It was nearing half-past when Wickham finally showed, and he looked the worse for wear. It seemed not only did he not nap, he did not partake in a change of clothing or a shave either. He had dark circles about his eyes and yawned profusely as he took his seat at the table.

'I have some news to report, gentlemen,' the constable said as the server poured our tea.

Holmes, with an eager look and a fresh countenance that a sleepless night could not seem to erase, said, 'Pray tell.'

'Well,' he began anxiously as he sipped the hot tea, 'there was a constable at the door to my flat upon my return this morning. It seems they had been trying to reach me all through the night. One of the constables over by

Braithwaite, John Mackay, looked in on a Gypsy camp that was setting up in the middle of the night and noticed one of the young men had a nice, leather bag that he was carrying around. An overnight bag.'

'Mr Darcy's bag!' I exclaimed.

'Precisely,' said Wickham. 'The man, Jimmy Biggins, no more than my age and maybe younger, said he had found it in the woods, but I suppose that is just what you would expect him to say.'

'Or that he *actually* found it in the woods,' remarked Holmes.

Wickham shrugged. 'He had no alibi for the time frame of the murder. His own kin would not even stick up for him, which is highly unusual. They take care of their own yet did not even offer to vouch for his whereabouts that night.'

'Where, exactly, was the bag found?' Holmes asked.

'A spot about half-way between where Mr Darcy was found and Keswick. According to Mr Biggins, he was setting up to snare a rabbit for supper yesterday, and it was just lying there in the underbrush about a hundred yards or so off the road.'

'That places both the body and the overnight bag fairly close to one another.'

'Less than a mile, I would say,' replied Wickham.

Holmes then pressed, 'Did he show you himself where he found the bag?'

'Not me, personally, Mr Holmes, but according to Mackay, the man took them right to it.'

'Did he seem hesitant as he did so?'

'I asked that very question, thinking that maybe the Gypsy was making things up as he went, and the reply was no, he seemed quite sure of himself. Nonetheless, Mackay did not believe he was being truthful. Anyone can say, "Yes, this is the spot." And, "Yes, I found it here"—his words, not mine.'

Holmes' expression soured. 'I wish you would have came and retrieved me once news of this broke. I should like to have been there myself.'

'I apologise, Mr Holmes, this all unfolded rather quickly, and I was still half-taken with sleep when they found me.'

Holmes waved the statement off. 'What's done is done.'

I could see the obvious frustration in Wickham's twisted brow. He went on, 'They had done all the legwork before I came on board, but I don't believe they asked the right questions. As far as Mackay was concerned, Biggins was the murderer so, in his eyes, there was no need for further questioning. So, I asked some of my own.'

'And did your questions shed any light on the matter?' my friend asked.

'Some. There is but one thing I can think of that will make a Gypsy family turn on one of its own, and that is courting a non-Gypsy. Mr Biggins affirmed my suspicion with some pressing. However, what he would not do is give up the young girl's name, even though she could alibi him out of trouble. He would only say she was from Appleby, and they had been secretly courting for the past two summers at the horse fair. This year, however, their courtship was cut short for she took a job as a housemaid here in Keswick.'

Holmes had finished his cup of tea and was pouring himself another. Without looking up from the task he offered, 'The Darcy's.'

'That is correct, Mr Holmes. They just brought on a new housekeeper a month ago. Mr Darcy brought home a new hunting horse, and Mrs Darcy brought home one Miss Annalisa Welby to help keep up with the growing and newly refurbished estate. I did not let on that I knew who his sweetheart was.'

I interjected, 'Why do we not ask Miss Welby ourselves? He may not give her up, but she may be willing to talk if it means sparing Mr Biggins' life.'

The young constable shook his chaotic riot of ginger curls. 'This is not the first time a Gypsy has taken a liking to someone outside their fold. It does not happen often, but it does happen. In every case one thing is a constant. The Gypsy makes the other swear an oath that their relationship be kept secret, at least initially. Admitting to one publicly would almost assuredly get them both ostracized from their respective communities, which, in the end, will happen anyway if their courtship results in marriage. I suspect since they would not vouch for him that his family has already somehow found out about the pair or at least suspect some sort of ill-advised dalliance.'

With Holmes in an introspective stare, no doubt putting these new pieces of this puzzle into their proper place, I took a sip of tea and asked, 'Could he also be our intruder?'

Wickham rubbed at his reddened eyes and yawned once again. I sympathized for I felt much the same way; I was not expecting my first night on holiday to be a sleepless one.

'It seems he was caught within an hour and a half of the break-in,' the constable finally said. 'It would be a jaunt, especially at night, but I think he could have made it from Muirhouse back to their camp in that time frame. However, according to Mackay, no keys of any kind were found on him or in the overnight bag.'

'He could have hidden it,' I interjected. 'That key was worth ten thousand pounds, and I would wager he was not keen to share it. That money was their ticket to a new life together away from the communities that were no doubt going to shun them once the relationship became public.'

With an impassive expression, Holmes replied, 'The key, Watson, was worth that great sum of money only to those who knew its particulars. Unless either the Gypsy or Miss Welby were privy to this information, there would have been no need to kill Mr Darcy for it. With Miss Welby only having been on staff but a month, I doubt she would have been entrusted with such knowledge so early into her employ. And let me also propose this: if both husband and wife had a key to access the money, who would be the easier target to be relieved of their key—a towering behemoth of a man or his smaller, weaker wife?'

We all sat quietly for a moment pondering that sobering fact. Being overcome with a combination of exasperation and weariness, I finally asked, 'So where does that leave us? Do we believe Mr Biggins had anything to do with the murder?'

'I do not,' replied Wickham in a defiant tone.

Holmes responded only with an off-centered grin. He then asked, 'Is there more to this story that would leave you incredulous?'

Wickham then explained with aplomb, 'Not more, so much as just not sitting right. In all honesty, Mr Holmes, merely having Mr Darcy's overnight bag, even for a Gypsy, is not enough to level a charge of suspicion of murder, yet that is exactly what has happened. Having now exhausted the conversation on the key, let us also not forget that no murder weapon was found, neither at their camp, where the man said he found the bag, nor at their previous campsite. Oh, they had small hatchets, big enough to chop kindling or a small sapling but nothing big enough or sharp enough to take a man's head off in one swipe. Biggins was arrested with the overnight bag in his hands. He made no attempt to hide it. What I want to know is if he did the deed and had the prize, why jaunt around with the useless overnight bag of the man you just killed out for all to see? Why did he not hide it when the constable arrived? Why did he even have it at all? With ten thousand pounds, he could have had as many overnight bags as he wanted. No, something is missing in all of this, of that I am sure. Nonetheless, my hands are tied.'

'How so?' I asked.

'Because as soon as they had the Gypsy behind bars, Mackay wired Chief Constable Dunne in Carlisle to tell him that he had snared the murderer. The man has always been a bit of an apple polisher and wanted to crow to our boss personally. At any rate, Dunne is especially hard on the Gypsies and though an honourable lawman, and recently knighted, as well, I believe his instinct is clouded by his hatred of the group—of that, he keeps no secrets. If this Biggins fellow really did this, further investigation will prove the point. But I fear if this were to go to the assizes, even only on assumptions and flimsy evidence, prejudice against the Gypsies and Dunne's good name will all but seal his fate while the real murderer goes free.'

Holmes looked upon the young constable satisfactorily. 'You have the makings of a decent detective, Constable Wickham, and that can only be good news to the people of Keswick. We must now work diligently to prove either Mr Biggins' innocence or his guilt.'

'And I am up for the challenge,' the young man replied.

I then remembered another question that needed to be answered that had yet been addressed and asked, 'What of whether Darcy made it to the train?'

'Ah yes,' Wickham responded. 'Completely slipped my mind last night. It seems that Mr Darcy indeed made the 1:30 p.m. to Workington. He bought his ticket at 1:20 p.m. and Mr Morrow, the station master, saw him get on the train.'

I could tell by the slight slackening of Holmes' features that he would have to abandon one of his theories, or at the very least revise it. Holmes never treated incorrect theories as obstacles, however. He always felt disproving one brought him all the more closer to the truth.

'What, then, shall our next move be?' asked the constable.

'It seems your hands will be full at present with the imminent arrival of the Chief Constable,' replied Holmes.

Wickham sighed resignedly. 'It is a very hard thing to do, indeed, knowing you two are on the hunt while I am forced down rabbit holes.'

'Our paths momentarily diverge, but they will converge tonight. Will you be able to pull yourself away to see Mrs Darcy off to Carlisle this afternoon?'

'That should not be a problem. Speaking of problems, I have already seen Mrs Dower on my way over here and per your request mentioned Mrs Darcy's sabbatical to Carlisle while Mr Darcy's funeral arrangements are being made. No doubt the news has been heard by half the village by now.'

'Excellent, just what we want,' Holmes replied with satisfaction as he drank the last of his tea. 'The more people who know the house will be absent its primary occupant the better. If the news makes it to our culprit's ear, he might be emboldened to strike sooner rather than later. Go. Do your employer's bidding for the day, even if the chief constable has you going down rabbit holes. But remember this,' he added enigmatically, 'one cannot rule a suspect in or out without evidence to support it. Do not be so quick to rule out the Gypsy. Not yet.'

'But the obvious fact is—'

Holmes cut Wickham off, 'There is nothing more deceptive than an obvious fact.'

Duly admonished, Wickham nodded, 'Of course.'

'Watson and I shall keep busy by paying Mrs McGlinn another visit. Much is transpiring around her, and it is worrisome to me that a woman with child is in the vicinity of such a reprehensible event. She has been spared thus far, but I am not sure for how much longer, a gun and a dog notwithstanding. I want to try and convince her to come to town and stay at the hotel until this affair is settled. If the Gypsy, Biggins, is the culprit, it should not take but a day or two to prove it. But a few days in a hotel room is worth two lives if the murderer still lurks.'

Wickham shook his head and smiled, 'It will be all for naught, Mr Holmes. I have known Morwenna McGlinn my entire life. Do not let the gigglemug and winks fool you (here, Holmes glanced at me with the slightest of grins). She may be a slight woman, but she has a fiery personality and is unflappable when she has put her mind to something.'

'If I am unsuccessful then I can leave her to her fate with a clear conscience. But I must try to relay to her the very real possibility of danger that staying there alone poses to her and her unborn child.'

We ate our breakfast and parted ways with Wickham, he to the constabulary to wait on word of the Chief Constable while Holmes and I walked out to the McGlinn place, the distance of about a mile once we made the outskirts of the village.

We finally turned onto the long, dirt path and made our way up the gentle slope to the cottage a few hundred yards up from the road. The place looked idyllic with bare, grey, spiked peaks as a backdrop and a mid-morning sun splashing shadows and sunshine alike along the dewy, cranesbill-covered meadow that separated the house from the road. I could easily see how someone could fall in love with such a place. But the Jekyll of warm, sunny skies is but one face of this area. I had yet to see the Hyde of endless, grey, chilled, rain-swept skies that would send one to the solace of Cornwall, as was the case of Mrs McGlinn.

Holmes was silent and introspective as we climbed the slope. Several times I noticed his eagle-like stare looking off into the wood line some fifty yards on either side of us. I knew my friend and his tendencies. His warning to Wickham notwithstanding, Holmes would not be so intent and taciturn if he truly thought the young man currently incarcerated was the murderer. No, I was sure the vile creature still prowled the hills somewhere out there, and Holmes would find him. It was at times like these that the great detective was at his best.

As we got closer, we could see Mrs McGlinn hanging a basket of laundry on the east side of the cottage, taking in the morning sun with her little terrier at her feet. At first, I thought they were sheets, but with a better look, I could see the sleeves dancing in the breeze. They were a man's shirts. Next, to her diminutive frame, they appeared much larger than they already were. Behind her was a fenced in area, presumably for the chickens—I did not see any larger animals. And the vegetable garden was on the west side, where it could get most of the afternoon sun and warmth. She saw us walking up the trail and waved. I was sure I could see her smiling.

Her little friend was about to pay us a visit with his high-pitched *yip*, but with a firm pat on her thigh and a pointed finger, the dog stayed put and watched us from afar.

She left her laundry and came down to meet us.

'I hope we are not intruding, Mrs McGlinn,' called out Holmes as she neared, and we tipped our hats in hello.

She revealed her ever-present smile and replied, 'Please, Mr Holmes, I would chase a butterfly if it would keep me from laundry. I am only doing some now because my husband is readying me for child rearing by hiding clothes under our bed. I do wish he had a bit cleaner manners, but men will be men, sir. His punishment will be that he'll be minus two shirts and a pair of trousers on his journey.'

'Yes,' Holmes agreed, 'I believe our landlady back at Baker Street would no doubt share your views on the ills of men's habits, would she not, Watson?'

'Well, at least one man's habits, anyway,' I admonished cheekily. Turning my head around to take in the beautiful backdrop I then said, 'What an absolutely spectacular view.'

Mrs McGlinn looked around her and nodded almost remorsefully. 'I will indeed miss the view, but not the weather. You are blessed to see the Lake District with rouge upon her cheeks. You must trust me when I say that she looks like a hag if ever there was one when the clouds lower and the winds howl, and the rain and cold take over. Yet on days like this, there is no prettier place on earth. But alas, Cornwall has a beauty of its own, so I will just replace one jewel for another.' She then looked at us directly and said, 'If I knew you were coming, I could have given you directions through the woods. There is a path that would have cut your trek in half. I take that into town rather than the road.'

Holmes said, 'We are none the worse for wear, madam. The warmth of the sun is much more refreshing than the shade of the wood. It was a pleasant walk.'

'So, you have thought of some more questions for me?' she asked as she wiped her hands on her threadbare summer dress.

Holmes replied, 'Not so much questions as supplications. May we go inside and talk?'

Her cheerfulness left her momentarily as she eyed each of us with a questioning glare but did not ask for clarification. She only winked, at last, and said as her smile returned, 'Well, I have never had the likes of a great detective from London in my home before, so if you do not pass judgment on my interior tastes you are more than welcome to come in.'

The home was small and cluttered but clean, all on one floor, as far as could be ascertained. There were a lot of bric-a-brac here and there, none of which I could readily make out in the wan light, and some sea-faring implements and a rolled-up length of rope, no doubt her husband's. The living area was a small, open place which shared its space with the kitchen. A roughly-hewn wood table, with only one chair on the kitchen side, separated the two spaces. Upon the right side of the table was an open cloth of butter and a knife, and on the left a meager half-loaf of bread—a testament to her only slightly better than hand-to-mouth existence, which rather saddened me. There was something about her, maybe her size, maybe her endless jollity despite what little she had that made me care perhaps more than I otherwise would. However, I digress. To the left of the table was a doorway, presumably to the bedroom. One cloth couch and well-worn chair next to the hearth rounded out what furniture there was. Mrs McGlinn sat in the chair, and my friend and I shared the couch. The dog curled up by the dying fire but kept his eyes firmly on us.

'So, what are these entreaties you wish to make upon me, Mr Holmes?' the woman finally asked with a curious grin as she poked the logs in the fire, sparking it back to life to chase the coolness from the room.

'There were developments overnight regarding Mr Darcy.'

Her eyes brightened. 'Did they catch the one responsible?'

'They have a Gypsy in custody. A Jimmy Biggins.'

She shook her head angrily. 'It does not surprise me. They are nothing but trouble, all of them. I am one chicken short, and you can bet it can be found in one of their pots. Gypsies are everywhere up and down the roads to Appleby this time of year.'

When Holmes did not immediately offer it, Mrs McGlinn asked, 'What evidence have they against this Biggins fellow?'

'He was found with Mr Darcy's overnight bag on his person.'

'Well, there you have it, sir,' she said with relief, 'proof of his guilt if ever there was.'

'For some, perhaps. My requirements for guilt are a bit more considerable.'

'Well, how did the scoundrel come by the bag then?' She wore an aggravated expression that looked misplaced upon her usually cheerful features.

'He said he found it in the woods not far from here.'

The woman's face pinched in confusion as she looked from one to the other of us.

'I'm afraid, Mrs McGlinn, that you seem to be in the middle of some unsavory happenings,' Holmes clarified. 'Mr Darcy's body was found just east of here, and his overnight bag in the woods between here and town. This, even though he was seen boarding a train to Workington, which is in the opposite direction on the coast. Now, more investigation may prove the Gypsy guilty, but if I am correct—and I usually am—then the murderer is still on the loose. Therefore, I implore you to rethink staying here. You have more than yourself to think about.'

'What makes you think the murderer will want to kill again?' she asked. 'Maybe Mr Darcy was targeted for his own unknown indiscretions and not necessarily some uncontrollable lust to kill on the part of the killer. Maybe he came upon something he was not supposed to see and met his end because of it. If that is the case, surely no one else will meet the same fate and all this worry is for nothing.'

Holmes leaned forward and looked upon her intently. 'That may be the case, Mrs McGlinn, but if there is any doubt, any at all, in the murderer's mind that the deed was committed in anonymity, then he will go about tying up what loose ends he deems fit to tie. And since you seem to be right in the middle of things, he might see fit to make sure you stay quiet, whether you actually saw anything or not.'

She was about to offer up a reply when suddenly, there came a furtive noise from somewhere in the home.

Even the dog's ears perked, but it only looked around and did not get up to investigate.

Holmes put his finger to his lips; however, it seemed that whatever we heard Mrs McGlinn had not. She asked, 'What is it, Mr Holmes? Did you hear something?' She looked around the room.

Suddenly, there were several great thuds and a crash that came from another room. We all rose quickly to investigate, and Mrs McGlinn knocked over a small stack of firewood next to the hearth as she reached for a game gun that was resting against the wall. As quickly as we could, we manoeuvered around the loose firewood and made haste to the to the room off the kitchen, which was the bedroom. The back window was open, and a nightstand lay knocked over. Holmes ran to the window with me at his back. About twenty feet from the back of the house was a thick stand of pines that led into the deeper stretch of woods that straddled the valley. We saw the tails of an un-tucked shirt quickly disappear between the evergreens.

Without warning, we heard Mrs McGlinn shout, 'Move!'

The barrel of the shotgun was thrust between us, and the room exploded in a horrific noise that left my ears ringing like cathedral bells. The shot went high clipping the tops of the twelve-foot pines.

'Come, Watson!'

'I will come, too!' Exclaimed Mrs McGlinn.

'No,' Holmes demanded. 'Stay in the house.'

'But I have the shotgun.'

'Yes, and your aim leaves something to be desired. Please stay here. I do not wish to be mistaken for the top of an evergreen.'

We ran out of the room and across the kitchen to a side door. Outside was a small porch with three steps, at the bottom of which was the basket and laundry. These we jumped and ran around the fenced-in area to the back of the house and into the thick of pines.

'Watson, you go there,' he pointed excitedly, 'And I shall go this way. Call if you see anything.'

We both made our way through the dense pines, whose branches in many places overlapped, making the way difficult. I could hear Holmes to my left shuffling about the trees. I tried to see ahead and to my right where the pines transitioned to ash and elm but saw and heard nothing. The blackguard had a full half-minute head start on us. If he knew his way around, he was too far ahead to catch.

After about thirty yards of meandering around and through pine trees, I finally came out the other side. There, I found Holmes scanning the area as he caught his breath. He had a few red welts on his cheeks most likely from some uncooperative branches. I joined him, searching the area around for movement. Some distance ahead was a wide stream and beyond that, the land rose to its barren summit not far off. It was clear that we were the only souls. There was nowhere to hide if the interloper had come this way through the pine thicket.

Holmes then gazed with disappointment at the woods that stretched well off into the distance to the east. He said, 'Let us get back to Mrs McGlinn in case our intruder has a mind to double back while we are out here looking for him.'

When we retraced our steps back through the pines, we were greeted by wide, blue eyes and the barrel of the shotgun, but once Mrs McGlinn saw that it was us, she lowered it.

'The Gypsies are getting audacious,' said Holmes sarcastically as we all walked around the enclosure and stopped at the small side porch.

'He must have thought he could rummage on the inside of the house while I was out here with the laundry,' Mrs McGlinn said as she kicked at the basket, shifting it in the grass. 'Probably after my bread and vegetables. He must not have planned for me to come back inside so soon.'

Holmes' eyes darted around eagerly as he spoke, 'Or he was waiting precisely for you to come back inside. But he did not expect you do to so with company.'

The woman relented with a sigh as she contemplated Holmes' meaning. 'You were right, Mr. Holmes. It is not safe here. But I do not know what to do. I have nowhere to go.'

Holmes responded, 'No friends or family?'

'I am an only child and my parents have been in the grave for the better part of ten years. My friends have as little or less room than I have here. I could not impose.'

'Would your employer be willing to accommodate you at the Royal Oak? It should only be a few days, and you would be safe there.'

She sniffled. It was the first time that I had seen fear on her face. 'But I have no money to pay for a room. My wages are just enough to pay the rent, and I won't see any money from my husband for some time yet.'

I spoke up. 'If your employer cannot spare a few days' accommodation for you, then I will tell him myself that I shall pay your bill.'

Her sunny smile returned once again, and she said, 'You are too kind, Dr Watson. If I were not so deprived of height, and you not so tall, I would kiss you on your cheek, sir.'

I repaid her with a quick, blushing beam of my own. 'It is our pleasure to help in any way we can, Mrs McGlinn.'

She ascended the stairs as she said, 'Just let me get a few things, and we can walk back to Keswick together.' She then turned to us and added sternly, 'I shall come out here every day, though, to feed my Bobby and the chickens.'

As she went back inside to retrieve some toiletries and a change of clothing, Holmes and I ascended the steps of the small porch and waited. It was then that I noticed his wide grin. 'And the smile you now wear is somehow at my expense?' I asked.

'What a perfect turn of phrase,' he said with a chuckle. 'The gratuity for which the woman works is growing, Watson. This trip may end up costing you dearly.'

7

Mrs McGlinn put her dog in the large enclosure with the ten or so chickens. It sniffed around the henhouse, growled once at the big box then whimpered, most likely due to its unwanted incarceration, and settled on a thick patch of hay in the far corner away from the pecking poultry.

Pointing her finger at the dog, Mrs McGlinn said, 'Now, you leave the chickens be, Bobby, and I shall come back to feed you and let you run a bit tomorrow.'

The terrier whined but seemed to sense that this was only a temporary inconvenience. It finally placed its head on its paws and just stared unblinkingly at us as she closed the gate.

We heard one more whimper as we walked away.

Mrs McGlinn and I chatted the entire walk back. Holmes, however, was silent. I could see as we walked that his knitted brow began to slacken. That could only mean he was beginning to untie the knot of this murder as he picked at it in that great brain of his. By the time we reached Keswick, he was almost ebullient.

At Holmes' behest, Mr Bruce, the owner of the Royal Oak, accommodated Mrs McGlinn in a small, spare room at the back of the inn, off the kitchen. He was a very agreeable fellow who was more than happy to help the great detective for no charge.

We said our goodbyes, and Holmes and I were on our way back to the King's Arms.

Holmes started, 'I think I fancy a trip to Workington, Watson. It seems all the threads I hold in this little affair either begin or end there.'

'I shall get a schedule at once,' I replied.

Holmes shook his head. 'No, Watson. I believe I need you here. I want you to see Mrs Darcy off, and Constable Wickham may look us up with any news of the Gypsy investigation. And although you may believe that Mrs McGlinn will stay put, something in her eyes told me that the last thing she wanted to do was leave her home. I want you to surreptitiously keep an eye on her in case she has plans to return home in our absence.'

'She has the will and the tenacity for self-defense,' I offered, 'however wielding a game gun almost as tall as she will make hitting anyone difficult unless they are directly in front of her.'

'You do not give her enough credit, Watson.' He offered. 'She missed the intruder on purpose.'

I was speechless. Holmes knew the revelation caught me off guard. 'Don't just see,' he added. 'Observe. Mrs McGlinn had no problems whatever holding the shotgun on us as we exited the trees after the chase. Perhaps she does not hold as much enmity towards the Gypsies as she would like us to believe.'

My eyes widened. 'The man *was* hiding in her bedroom. Do you think she is having an affair with a Gypsy while her husband is away at sea? Could it be that the child is not her husband's?'

'It is possible; however, it does not have to be as dramatic as that. It could be that the chicken she mentioned being pilfered was perhaps actually given.'

'You mean she is helping them?'

'It is one option among many. Data, data, data, Watson. I need clay to make bricks.'

'Wickham has already stated that prejudice towards them ran rampant in these parts,' said I. 'If townsfolk knew she was abetting Gypsies, it would not go well for her.'

Holmes gave no reply but instead changed the subject. 'It may be late before I return tonight. It seems the last train back from Workington is late afternoon. If I am not done with my inquiries, I may have to employ a coach for my return. At any rate, if I am not back by the late train, it may not be until closer on midnight before I return. I trust that I will not miss much in the few hours I am absent. In fact, nothing at all may happen the first night Mrs Darcy is out of the house. My hopes are, however, that the intruder will not wish to delay getting their hands on that money. If that is indeed the case, I would not think anything should happen before the darker hours after midnight.'

At one p.m. I left Holmes talking to the station master and went back to the King's Arms. Beforehand, I took it upon myself to pay a young hotel steward at the Royal Oak to keep an eye on Mrs McGlinn and to come and get me at the lakeshore should Mrs McGlinn feel the need to leave the premises.

I obtained from my room one of the journals I thought I would be neglecting on hearing the word *murder*, and made my way down to the shore of Derwentwater. I found a shaded bench near the pebbly shore, took up roost, and I made a feeble attempt at reading it. I will freely admit that it was not nearly as engaging as investigating the decapitation of one of the landed gentry with the possible implication of Gypsies.

After only a few moments, I put the journal down and went over things as I saw them, which seemed the more prudent use of my time. The first thing that struck me as I pondered the events was that there seemed to be a lack of suspects. No one seemed to have it in for Mr Darcy. Not locally, anyway. Maybe Holmes would find something more substantial with his inquiries in Workington.

And what of the Gypsy, Jimmy Biggins? He was found with Mr Darcy's bag, and it seemed he had help on the inside of the Darcy home with his love interest Annalisa Welby. Could they have conspired to do her master in and take the money from the safe to start a new life away from the Gypsies, who obviously were not inclined to take in as family someone from the outside?

There was really no one else that came to my mind. The wife seemed genuinely distraught at the whole affair. Though I believe with her rugged American individualism, she certainly had the fortitude to carry out something like murder, I found it difficult picturing her wielding an implement hefty enough for a decapitation. And I just did not see what her motive could have been to do such a terrible thing.

I finally determined that the answer had to be in Workington, and if anyone could find the thread that held this mystery together it would be Sherlock Holmes.

It was about this time that I saw a group of constables, along with a taller, older officer walking toward a boat launch where a dozen or so boats were lapping in the lake water. Constable Wickham noticed my wave, and he said something to the taller gentleman and made his way over to me.

'Hello, Dr Watson,' said Wickham. He looked only marginally better than he had at breakfast.

I offered a greeting in reply then asked, 'So what is all this about?'

He looked back at the group of men. 'The taller one is Chief Constable Dunne. He has just finished interviewing Jimmy Biggins. It did not go well.'

'He did not confess to the murder, did he?'

'Oh, no, nothing like that. But as I feared, Dunne is certain that the Gypsy did it. I was present for the interrogation, so I am perplexed as to where he got the idea, but Dunne thinks the head is in Derwentwater. In his eyes, the lake would be the most obvious place to discard something as unwanted as a human head. He is organizing boats to drag the lake.'

'At this point, what will finding Mr Darcy's head accomplish, besides giving Mrs Darcy a whole body to bury?'

Wickham shrugged his shoulders as the Chief Constable bellowed ferociously, 'Wickham! We need you here, lad, not over there!'

'I can only do what he says to do. Unfortunately, I do not think I will be available to see Mrs Darcy off. Holmes wanted me at the station to see her onto the train, but I fear that plan is for naught. Give her my condolences, will you?'

'Certainly.'

He turned to leave then turned back. 'Where is Holmes, by the way?' he asked.

'Inquiring in Workington,' I replied.

The constable nodded. 'Exactly where I should be right now,' he said with exasperation.

'Wickham!' came the cry again.

I nodded for him to go. 'You don't want to lose your situation. Go. We will meet up tonight. Come to the hotel when you can. I shall be there. Holmes may be late, but the plan shall go off regardless.'

Wickham nodded and said over his shoulder as he trotted off, 'I shall not miss that for the world.'

8

Four hours of poking and prodding the lake with some twenty boats proved fruitless. After only a quarter of that time, I grew bored watching the fiasco and went back to the hotel but not before stopping off at the Royal Oak to see how my charge was doing. The steward had been checking up on her every hour on the pretense that Sherlock Holmes insisted she be looked after in her condition, asking if she needed anything to eat or drink or a book to read, the latter of which she finally acquiesced to. Mrs McGlinn read for a while, then having grown tired of that, decided to take a nap. That was her current situation.

I returned to the King's Arms, got a bite to eat, then walked back to Muirhouse. Alfred was loading the last of three large pieces of luggage onto the back of a cab, which would then deposit Mrs Darcy at the train station for the afternoon train to Carlisle.

'Good afternoon, Mrs Darcy,' said I as she came through the front entrance bedecked in black and wearing a face as dark as her attire. Yet hidden between the lines of that beautiful face, ruddy and weary from crying, was a defiance that was almost palpable.

'Are you absolutely sure this is the right thing to do?' she questioned as I took her hand gently in greeting. Her voice was sterner and less sombre than the previous day. Anger at her loss was heightening.

'I have been an associate and close friend to Sherlock Holmes for many years, and if I have learned anything in that time it is that there is good reason to do whatever he asks.'

'I am not a shrinking violet, Dr Watson. I know how to hold my own. I was born and bred that way, despite my social standing.'

'Of that, I have no doubt, madam, but you must trust us this one time. We do not know if the intruder was indeed your husband's murderer or not. We also do not know, as yet, where all these paths lead, and I can assure you, Mrs Darcy, that Holmes and I have seen lesser crimes than this lead to wells of malevolence, the depths of which have never been fully plumbed.'

She was quiet for a moment, then a wave of acquiescence washed over her features. 'Of course, you are right, Dr Watson. I will do as Mr Holmes asks. Speaking of which, where is the man?'

I helped her into the cab. 'Holmes never tires until the criminal is in the dock. He is out flushing more clues. He and Constable Wickham both send their regrets for not being here to send you off.'

She smiled weakly. 'I would rather they be out there finding the murderer of my husband than here feeling sorry for the poor, grieving widow. Action is always better than observation. My father always said that to me. Keeping true to that statement is what made him wealthy. If I have learned anything from him, it is that.'

'If all goes well, we will be wiring you in a day or two with good news.'

'Thank you.'

I closed and patted the door twice loudly, and the cab slowly lumbered down the drive.

Alfred came up from behind, and as we both watched, he asked, 'What is the plan now, sir?'

I replied, 'In case we are being watched, I shall now leave. You and the staff do your normal duties, as you would anytime the house is left empty of its owners. When you lock up for the night, leave the front door unlocked. Holmes, Wickham, and I will enter there, as that door faces the lake, and it should shield us from the wood, from which the burglar will most likely strike. Holmes does not believe that anything will take place until the darkest hours before dawn, but we will be in place long before that. Then, it is just a waiting game. Do not come out of your rooms for anything, regardless of what you might hear unless summoned by us directly. Make sure the rest of the staff knows that. Their life might depend upon it.'

I could tell that Alfred was visibly shaken. 'I do not think that will be a problem, Doctor.'

. . . . .

I was nearing the town hall on my way back to the hotel when my little steward boy looking after Mrs McGlinn came running up to me. 'Sir, sir! It is Mrs McGlinn.'

'What is it, boy?' I asked, taken aback.

He gulped heavily. 'Well, she has been sleeping all afternoon, after reading, which I already told you, but I decided to check up on her again. I knocked, but she would not wake up and answer the door. Well, it's not something I normally do, but I put my eye to the keyhole. I could see her under the covers, but she wasn't moving. I came here straight away since you are a doctor. If there is something wrong with her, a doctor is the first person who should know.'

'Thank you,' said I with concern.

We both dashed the few streets to the Royal Oak, passed the reception desk and through the dining area and kitchen to the little room in the back.

I knocked loudly on the door. 'Mrs McGlinn, it is Dr Watson. Is everything alright?'

There was no answer.

'I am coming in.' I tried the knob, but it was locked. I slammed my bulk against the door, and after two attempts, it splintered open. I rushed to her bedside. There was no movement of her body whatsoever, and I knew that I was already too late to save her. Pregnancy is such a blessing, but with it comes countless curses, all of which can snuff out the mother's life. In her attempt to bring a life into the world, Mrs McGlinn had ended up losing two for her trouble.

I slowly bent down and felt the body. It was cool and soft. Too soft. I pulled back the covers, and what was before my eyes was a pillow and a few extra blankets made up to look like a person under the covers. I had been duped. Holmes would either laugh at me for my folly or admonish me for my miscarriage in not following his directives; I have come to loath either of those reactions.

To the left of the door was a window, which led to a small mews between the rows of buildings. It was open, and the curtains fluttered softly in the breeze.

'It looks like she fooled us both,' the boy said, trying to hide a smile.

'Indeed, she has,' I replied in frustration.

The robust Mr Bruce, the owner of the Royal Oak, appeared in the doorway wearing an angry face. 'What is the meaning of all this? Do you often go about breaking down doors of people who are trying to help in an investigation?'

'I apologise, Mr Bruce. She was not answering the door, and in her state, I thought she was having complications with her pregnancy. I tried the knob, but it was locked. I did not have time to search out a key, so I forced my way in.'

The big man looked at the crumpled bedding and laughed. 'It looks like little Morwenna got the best of you, she did.'

A bit wounded, I said, 'I will obviously pay for the damages.'

'Of course, you will, Dr Watson. I know you and Mr Holmes are good for it. Besides, this will make a terrific story. When word gets about, I'll be having to turn people away from my little inn, it'll be so busy.'

'Where do you think she went?' the boy asked.

'More than likely back home,' said I. 'She does not scare easily, I give her that.'

'Living with that husband of hers should callus just about any soft feelings,' said Bruce.

'What do you mean by that?' I asked.

He put his hands up defensively. 'I will only say that they are both a pair of odd ducks. Anything else is gossip in which I refuse to partake. I will say that getting little Morwenna to do something she does not want to do is as easy as pulling out your own teeth.'

I shrugged as I peered out the window into the street. 'Well, if home is where she prefers, I shall not endeavour to keep her from it. I have other, more pressing things for which to prepare.'

. . . . .

When I finally returned to the King's Arms, there was a telegram awaiting me. It was from Holmes. It read thus:

This little puzzle is coming together splendidly. Lots to share. Will not be home on the late train but will be home well before midnight. I have a coach on standby to leave as soon as I have finished here. An hour and a half of travel and I will be back at Keswick. Do not wait for me. I will go straight to Muirhouse upon arriving.

And of course, that is all Holmes would relay to me. He preferred to keep people in the dark until that penultimate point which would bring the largest amount of awe. He was the lead actor in these little dramas and refused to give away the ending until his audience was at the height of anticipation. As part of the audience, I would have to wait.

It was about this time that Constable Wickham rushed into the lobby.

'You have got news,' I anticipated.

'And not good, unfortunately,' was his winded reply. 'While we were out dragging the lake for a head that never materialized, Jimmy Biggins managed to pick the lock to his cell. He must have had implements hidden in his shoes for Mackay swears he was searched before being locked up. We needed all the men we could spare for this little endeavour and only left one officer. Mr Biggins snuck out the back where we had examined Mr Darcy's body while the officer up front was otherwise occupied.'

'What do you think his next move will be?'

'I saw the fear in his eyes as Chief Constable Dunne was interrogating him. My guess is he has had enough of this whole affair. He will hide out until nightfall then sneak back into the fold of his Gypsy family. He will swear off his dalliance with Annalisa Welby for the sake of his freedom, and they will leave the area as fast as they can strike their camp.'

'That is a good thing if he is not actually responsible for the death of Mr Darcy,' I replied.

'But you forget, Dr Watson, that Dunne *does* believe he is guilty and will not let him get away. As we speak, they are forming an ambuscade around the perimeter of the Gypsy camp and will lie in wait till he shows himself. I was only afforded the opportunity to come back to town to get a few able bodies to help secure the perimeter.'

'So that means you will not be with us tonight then?' I asked.

'It is not looking so.' I could see the disappointment on his face when he then said, 'The one time in my life that I was able to work with the great Sherlock Holmes, and it is all being ruined by a love-sick Gypsy who was in the wrong place at the wrong time.'

9

By 9:30 p.m. it was sufficiently dark for me to make my way to Muirhouse on my own. Holmes had not yet arrived, however, I expected him shortly based on his telegram. The night was broodingly dark, for clouds began gathering across the sky in the late afternoon and thickened as afternoon turned to evening. Wind whipped about, racing the clouds in from the west. The moon winked in and out as they shot across its face, and I had to forcibly keep my bowler from flying off my head as I walked. Far off thunder cut through the winds; it seemed inclement weather would finally descend upon the Lake District, and it would descend with a vengeance.

The front door was unlocked, as instructed, and I made my way into the dark and quiet house. It had a haunting allure with shadows clinging everywhere like tar. I wore soft-soled shoes to keep the echoes to a minimum as I spied a place to wait for Holmes. I wanted to be near the front door, so he would not have to venture to find me and we in our blindness might think the other was the burglar. I decided on the landing at the top of the stairs before it turned ninety degrees and ventured up the rest of the way to the first floor. There was also a window here, so I could look out onto the grounds near the carriage house and stable, as well as look down at the front entrance. Here is where I kept my vigil.

It was not long, perhaps a half-hour, before a furtive noise from somewhere in the house caught my attention, the soft steps of one on the stairs. Then, I remembered Alfred telling us that the servants quarters had a separate stairway at the back of the home for coming and going from their rooms upstairs without being seen. I was about to investigate when movement outside caught my attention. I saw the shadow of a woman, her long dress fluttering in the wind. Whoever it was must have crept down the back stairs and exited through the back mudroom. I could only see her briefly before she disappeared behind the small stable at that back of the house; however, in that fleeting moment I could see she was carrying something. I waited anxiously to see if she would reappear at the other end of the stable for she seemed headed in the direction of the woods closest to the property on the north-east side of the home.

While I waited, luck was on my side, as the bright summer moon shone through a large patch of cloudless sky, which brightened the landscape. I only hoped it would not disappear behind the clotting storm clouds before she re-emerged on the other side of the stable. And it was during this interlude that I noticed a small light, probably a candle, glittering in and out back in the recesses of the tree line. Someone was waiting. They were, more than likely, continually placing their hand across its face to keep the candle from being blown out in the unruly wind.

At this time, I surmised the candle holder to be the Gypsy boy, and the woman to be Miss Welby. Wickham had thought wrong when he proposed that the young man would give up so easily on love. The two would make their escape to better lives, while the police force was on a fool's errand.

When I finally saw the shadow emerge from the back of the stable, and just before the moon was lost permanently behind the gathering tempest, I had just enough light to see that the girl was carrying a small sack, the bottom of which was rounded and bulging. I cannot say for certain why, but the contents reminded me of a familiar shape, and it made my blood chill at the thought. The contents had the shape of a head!

I did not know my way around the home well enough to trace the young woman's steps, so I lunged down the steps two at a time then raced out the front entrance and around the house. I did not yet have a plan of action, only that I could not let them escape. I could not for the life of me tie either to the murder, but if the damning proof was in that sack she carried I would make sure they did not escape, and the particulars could be ascertained later.

With my best estimate, I entered the tree line where the two would have met. I squinted into the darker shadows and, after a moment, caught sight of the flickering light and pressed on, being as quick and stealthy as I could. The heavens helped me in that regard as the peels of once-far-off thunder were now directly upon Keswick and Derwentwater. Their angry tolls reverberated off the Cat Bells and Skiddaw mountains.

As I made my way towards them, I could not help but think my eyes were playing tricks on me. I watched their tarry shadows ahead of me meandering through the trees, yet whenever the lightning flickered across the sky, I thought I was seeing more moving shadows ahead and to my left. Did they have compatriots, come to help in their escape? I decided that they were shadows of branches and brush being whipped about in the winds for every shadow now seemed to be alive. I also wondered as I closed in, what were they going to do with the head? If it was hidden, it could have remained so, while they made their escape. Why take it with them? Again, it was a question that could be answered at a later time.

They had traversed a few hundred yards through the copses when a jagged spear of lightning was thrust down from the heavens and pierced Derwentwater some distance to my left. It looked like a fireworks display, and the thunder, almost immediately on its heels, was deafening. My ears were ringing, and my eyes were readjusting to the sepulchral darkness that followed when I felt someone from behind me reach around and clamp a leather-gloved hand over my mouth.

. . . . .

I tried mightily to resist, but the lock on me was like iron chains. I struggled, but it got me nowhere. Finally, completely at his mercy, the brute then whispered in my ear, 'Watson, it's me, Holmes. Do not make a sound when I let you go.'

Once free, I turned around. Holmes' tall, thin shadow stood before me with a smaller shadow at his back. I paid no mind to the lesser adumbration but focused my angst on my friend. I whispered, but my fury was palpable. 'Holmes, what in the devil are you doing, accosting me like that? You scared me half to death!'

'I could not risk you catching up to young Mr Bigging and Miss Welby.'

'And why not?' I asked in a frustrated hush. 'You did not see what Miss Welby left with. She is carrying a sack that I believe has the head of poor Mr Darcy. They are making their escape now.'

Holmes chuckled under his breath. 'Why do you think she carries Mr Darcy's cranium about?'

'I do not have the faintest clue, but I saw her sneak away from Muirhouse with a sack that was rounded at the bottom and looked quite heavy.'

'Rounded like, say, a teapot?'

I then knew where Holmes was going with the question, and suddenly felt ridiculous. This whole affair had me wrapped in its grasp and I was beginning to see what I wanted to see and not what was actually before me.

He patted me on the back. 'Come. I picked up Constable Wickham on my way back to Keswick. Let us get back to Muirhouse and get ready for our night and let poor Mr Biggins and Miss Welby go. The contents of the sack were more than likely a silver set with a teapot at the bottom that they will pawn for some much-needed money. I normally would not let such things pass, but I must let the smaller fish swim by as I wait for the bigger catch. Besides, I am quite certain that if it is Mrs Darcy's silver, she can afford to replace it, and if it Mr Darcy's silver, he no longer has need of it.'

As we quietly made our way back to the manor house, struggling against the wind, I asked Wickham, 'How did Holmes manage to snag you from your guard?'

'I was one of two that laid in wait along the road, in case Biggins had an inclination to travel so boldly. We stopped Holmes' carriage as it came through, and it didn't take much to convince me to abandon my sentry. My career be damned, I am not letting this murderer go free while we harass the innocent.'

'Bravo,' said Holmes enthusiastically. 'And I believe that this insubordination will be well worth the trouble. Come, let us set our trap.'

As we made the entrance to Muirhouse, the first raindrops began to fall.

. . . . .

We all made our way back to the billiard room and took up roost at the near, left corner of the room to be near both the light switch next to the doorway and the back window. Holmes intuited that in the burglar's haste, they would head to the right and around the billiard table and never notice our presence for the safe was at the opposite corner of the large room.

'How did you even know I was in the woods?' I asked, nodding to Wickham for some help.

Wickham placed a pistol I was unaware he was carrying on the billiard table. He then replied as he and I moved the rather heavy plaster bust away from the window and a possible premature fall that would no doubt wake the entire house, 'We saw you leave the house in such a rush, we feared the burglary had happened sooner than Mr

Holmes anticipated, so we rushed into the woods from the lane in hopes of cutting you off and giving chase together.'

'It was during one of the lightning displays,' Holmes added, 'that we were close enough that I could make out the couple. From there, I deduced you were on their trail thinking they were the murderers, so we endeavoured to stop you before you hindered their getaway.'

'So, what did you find out in Workington?' I finally asked, giving in to the anticipation I had been feeling since receiving his telegram.

A flash of lightning brightened up the room fleetingly, and at that moment, I could see that Holmes' austere features were more serious than usual. He turned to the window to watch and replied, 'I found out this whole affair has not been as it seemed from the very beginning. There were tell-tale signs I had picked up along the way, but many pieces were still missing. My trip to Workington filled in several important gaps, and I deduced the most logical suspect from what was left.'

'Well, who is it, man? Do you know who killed Mr Darcy?'

The sigh in reply told me that the answer would not be forthcoming. Holmes' histrionic flair was extremely irritating to those left out of the loop of his logic...which meant he irritated everyone. He was about to offer some sort of reply, to no one's satisfaction, I presumed, when his features straightened and stiffened. Though I could not see his face, I could tell my friend was smiling. 'I would rather show you, Watson. The rain has roused him from his lair earlier than I anticipated, but here comes our rat now.'

At the back, south corner of the property was a walking trail that led up to the Castlerigg stones a few miles away. We could see in the quick flashes of lightning an inky figure emerging from the trail and walking— with rather a profound equanimity—in our direction.

'Wickham, ready your pistol but keep it pointing down,' Holmes whispered. 'The scoundrel has been shot at and missed once, already, and I do not wish his luck to change until he is in the dock.'

'Right.'

'He should enter through the library, as he did the first time. We shall let him have free rein till he makes his way in here and to the safe. Then we shall have him.'

Holmes watched for what seemed an eternity but was probably no more than a minute or two. In that interim, the only thing I heard was the steady thrum of rain and quickening breaths of expectation.

My friend suddenly retreated quickly from the window sliding his back against the wall. 'He is coming this way! Hurry, put the bust back in its place!' said Holmes as he reached the doorway then fell back into the deeper darkness of the hall.

We did not have time to question why it mattered, so we did as Holmes commanded, and Wickham and I hurriedly began to manage the bust back into its place in front of the window. As we slid it across the carpeting, the edge of the base caught on my foot, and the bust began to sway. I could tell by the large arc the bust would be hard pressed to stay upright, but when Wickham lost his step, as well, and stumbled slightly forward, the bust fell entirely from its perch.

10

I heard a collective gasp as the bust descended to the floor. One of two things would happen: either the piece would break into a million fragments, or it would bounce with a thud upon the thick carpeting. Either scenario would notify the intruder of our whereabouts, and the trap would fail. I did the only thing I could think to do—I dove down, arcing my arms into a cradle, hoping to catch the thing before it hit. I closed my eyes and prayed for the right outcome.

My significantly softer body hit the floor with very little noise, and the bust landed embraced in my arms with nary a sound. Any disturbance within was no doubt deadened by the storm without...at least that is what I hoped.

I could sense more than see the shadowed intruder at the window above me. My racing heart thumped loudly in my ears, and I feared he would hear it above the din of the storm. Wickham was lost in the darkness somewhere to my right, and Holmes was in the safety of the still-darker hallway. All I could do was keep my place just below the window and pray he neither heard the near-disaster nor noticed me on the carpet below.

The would-be burglar tarried only a moment, taking in what I was hoping he believed was an empty room, then I could hear his soggy footsteps walking slowly away.

Holmes quickly and quietly re-entered the room. 'Splendid job, Watson,' he whispered. 'You saved us from a sure calamity. One, of course, entirely of your making.'

'Thank you for reminding me,' I murmured sardonically.

Wickham appeared from the shadows. 'That was a close call. I could not tell by his actions if he suspected anything or not. Do we think he is still coming as planned, or do we give chase?'

Holmes replied, 'He is lost to us by now if we had to give chase. By his actions, I predict he noticed nothing, or he would have run and not walked from the window. Hurry, everybody back into our positions and pray that we hear footsteps in the next few minutes.'

As expected, not long in waiting, we could hear soft footsteps coming down the hall. I anticipated hearing the dripping of wet clothes, but hearing nothing, I assumed he discarded his rain gear in the library to be quietly re-donned on his way out.

Holmes was in the corner, once more, while I and Wickham, pistol in hand, knelt behind the billiard table. Presently, a shadow, darker than the room, entered. He stopped just inside the doorway as if judging whether he was truly alone. It was an uncomfortably long moment before he finally made his way around the billiard table and to the back of the room. There was a brief flash of lightning and a low, far-off rumble of thunder. At that instant, we could see he had his back to us. In his right hand he held a large sack. With his left hand he took a chain from around his neck and pulled back the painting.

Suddenly, the light came on and Holmes said, 'Good evening, Mr Darcy.'

The large man turned on us, wide-eyed, but with not nearly as much surprise as both Wickham and myself.

Wickham showed his pistol but did not point it. His look was one of utter confusion as he looked from the man back to Holmes then back again. 'Mr Darcy? But...but you are dead.'

Holmes cut in, 'Someone is dead, yes.'

Robert Darcy wore much the same features as Wickham and me as he quietly eyed the three of us. Dark, wavy hair was plastered down over his forehead, and beads of rain still trickled their way down his chiseled nose and chin. As the astonishment wore off, his countenance then took on the features of a dejected child who had been caught with his hand in the cookie jar. He asked, 'How did you know?'

Holmes patted a leather smoking chair near to us on the inside wall of the room near a stand of billiard sticks. 'Please, come and take a seat while we sort out this whole affair.'

Wickham, whose features were slowly transforming from astonishment to anger, waved him on with the barrel of his pistol. 'I don't know what is transpiring here, Mr Darcy, but you have some explaining to do.'

Holmes put up a hand. 'I should like to set out the facts as I see them, and Mr Darcy can tell me where I have strayed. Please, Mr Darcy—sit.'

The big man sat as instructed, pushing nervously at the creases in his rain-spotted trousers. His hands shook almost uncontrollably.

Holmes began. 'This first question shall shed light on all else. You and Mrs McGlinn are lovers, yes?'

Mr Darcy would not look any of us in the eye. He only shook his head, yes. 'It did not start out as such, but yes, for the better part of a year, now.' His voice was almost a whisper and with its bass timbre was difficult to hear. Apparently, realizing the apprehensive quality of his voice, he cleared his throat.

I almost felt sorry for the man, except there was still a dead body which needed to be accounted for.

Wickham admonished, 'What about your poor wife, man? She loved you and gave you all of this,' he said with a sweep of his arm around the lavish room.

Mr Darcy looked upon Wickham with dark and pleading eyes. His voice was louder yet still retained his penitent tone when he replied, 'I know what Patricia has done for me. More than I deserve. I tried, lord knows I tried, but a man is not love's sovereign but its servant. My master felt compelled to chain me happily to Morwenna.'

'And the unborn child—yours?' Holmes asked.

Mr Darcy only nodded in the affirmative.

'All is as I suspected, thus far,' my friend replied.

Wickham did not know my friend as well as I, and he was obviously not taking into account the tomes I had written chronicling just how precisely Holmes conducted his interrogations when he cut in. Rage, and possibly embarrassment of the almost successful ruse, began to show. He demanded angrily, slapping his free hand on the billiard table, 'Who was it that lay in my constabulary with his head cut off? That is what I want to know!'

Holmes held up a finger to quiet Mr Darcy's response as he looked upon Constable Wickham. 'Do not ask the answer to a question that you yourself have the capability of answering with just a bit of consideration.'

'You act as though I already know,' Wickham replied.

You do, and with some prompts, I shall show you. Do you remember the answer you gave when I queried whether the dead man was Mr Darcy?'

He nodded. 'I said something to the effect that there are only a handful of people who had the height of Mr Darcy in the entire Lake District.'

'Who would those individuals be?'

Brow twisted in thought, Wickham replied, 'There is Chief Constable Dunne, but even he is a full inch or two under Darcy. There is Mr Finch, but he is much older, frailer, and arthritis has him in a permanent hunch. Leland Whitehill might be close. Then there is George McGlinn, but he...' His voice trailed off. 'But he is out to sea.' He looked at Holmes. 'Isn't he? I mean he might be the only man that is close in age and size to Mr Darcy.' This time he did not ask but stated as he eyed Mr Darcy, fury in his eyes, 'It was George McGlinn!'

Holmes was about to interject further, however, there was a sudden, loud *clap* that rang out from somewhere outside, startling us. I, having previously placed the bust back upon the stand, thus proceeded to knock it from its perch once again. It fell to the floor with a thud but did not break.

Our initial, collective thought was that it was just another clap of lightning; however, its timbre was higher pitched and much closer. We then simultaneously noticed the webbed hole in the window and quickly re-fixed our gaze upon Mr Darcy. He was slumped back awkwardly in the chair, craning his neck as if looking at the ceiling. Holmes grabbed him and pulled the man forward, and it was then we all noticed the small red hole in his forehead.

'Watson, attend to Mr Darcy if you can. Wickham, come with me!'

The two raced from the room, as I attended to the injured man. I felt for a pulse and found none, which is what I expected. It was a virtual impossibility to survive a bullet to the brain. There are rare cases of surviving gunshot wounds or partial impalements to the head. Usually, the location and depth of penetration were leading factors in whether the blow was fatal—that and blind luck. In this case, Mr Darcy's luck had run out. His lifeless eyes still wore their last pitiful stare. I gently closed them. Somehow, Mr

Darcy was now dead for the second time, shot by what looked to be a small calibre firearm.

I turned out the light so as not to telegraph my movements and become the target of a second volley, then crept to the window but kept my frame as best I could against the wall. Threads of rain fell from the sky and pinged at the window as I surveyed the saturated night. I saw nothing. The deliverer of the fatal shot was now gone.

Feeling the danger had passed, I turned the light back on as I waited for their return. Lacking anything else to do, I picked up the wayward bust and placed in on its stand for the second time. A small piece of the man's ear had indeed broken off in the fall. As I did this, I realized why Holmes wanted the bust placed back by the window. He knew it was Mr Darcy—for how long, I did not know—and the master of the house would have known about the bust in front of the window. If he had noticed it misplaced he might have become suspicious and left without trying for the money. My best guess was that the rain-streaked glass and darkness prevented a clear inspection of the room. I suspected nerves might have played a role, as well.

Within a few minutes, both men were back dripping unremittingly upon the polished floor. They each gave me a questioning look, although I am sure both already knew the answer. I, in return, replied only with a sombre nod.

'No luck catching the blackguard, then?' I stated more than queried.

'The blackguard was on horseback,' Holmes replied, as he and Wickham squeezed rain from their clothes, 'and *she* was very skillful at its handling in the rain.'

'Wait, what? A woman?' I was flabbergasted.

'Yes. I could see her hem flailing as she rode. But she was clever enough to keep a low profile, so I could not tell by size to whom the dress belonged. And though I cannot say with certainty, the beast looked to be absent of both saddle and bridle. My guess is it was quickly procured from the stable for a speedy extrication once the weapon was discharged.'

He then turned to Wickham. 'Is Mrs McGlinn a proficient rider?'

'A very good one in her youth,' he replied in a tone lost between exasperation and fear. 'But I daresay I haven't seen her ride in quite some time and certainly not bareback.'

'With or without a saddle, she risks injury to both herself and her baby by riding in her state,' I interjected.

'*If* Morwenna McGlinn was indeed the rider,' Holmes added, 'I think it was a risk she would have been willing to take to keep Mr Darcy from implicating her in any of this.'

I became confused by Holmes' uncertainty of the rider's identity and asked, 'If the rider was female, and it was *not* Mrs McGlinn, then who else could she be?'

Holmes gave me a telling look. 'Do not think for a second, Watson, that getting from Carlisle to Keswick and back in an evening is an impossibility. Even on a night such as this.'

The morass of deception, hate, and revenge seemed to be mounting even as the storm was finally beginning to ebb, and I could not seem to wrap my mind around any of it.

'Wickham. Go and release your compatriots from their uselessness,' Holmes said. 'There are much more fruitful tasks needing to be done. As quickly as you can. Then come to the McGlinn house. If Mrs McGlinn is not the rider then she is no doubt still waiting for the return of Mr Darcy and his small fortune. If she is the rider, I doubt she will return home. A diminutive, pregnant bareback rider should be easily spotted once the sun rises. Once you arrive, I believe a head and a sword shall need to be extricated from the hen house.'

11

Mr Darcy's hunting horse was found riderless trotting through the streets on the edge of town near both a path that Wickham said led through the wood to the McGlinn property and the road that led out of Keswick, up the eastern side of Bassenthwaite Lake and onto Carlisle. At that point, it was still anyone's guess as to which of the women had killed Mr Darcy, although I am quite sure Holmes knew. But knowing and proving were not birds of the same feather in the eyes of the law.

When Chief Constable Dunne and his assemblage of constables finally arrived from their soggy vigil, he was appreciative of our help in the matter thus far but did not wish us to take further part in any inquiry once he was finally put on the correct path. Holmes and I had to stay roadside while they investigated the McGlinn property. She was still inside waiting for the return of Mr Darcy, and George McGlinn's head and an antique broadsword was indeed found buried in the hay inside the hen house, just as Holmes had said. That is as much as we could glean before we were asked to vacate the area entirely as this was now solely a police matter. It seemed not everyone in this part of the country was a fan of having a consulting detective around, especially so for the people whose job was in detecting.

Wickham told us to meet him at the Royal Oak at noon for lunch, and he would apprise us of what we had missed. This time, Wickham was on time. He walked with purpose but looked dishevelled and weary. We all were. Even Holmes, for once, looked a bit rough around the edges, which is why strong coffee was all that was at the table.

He sat next to me and poured himself a cup of coffee from the carafe. 'Morwenna is a fighter,' he started. 'She will say nothing and has requested counsel. Dunne did all he could to break her, and despite his rather abrading personality, she was having none of it.'

'Yes,' Holmes replied, 'I think I have found my match in a personality that rubs people the wrong way.'

'And that is saying something,' I mused.

Holmes went on. 'What of Mrs Darcy? Did they send word to Carlisle to see if she was at the Rutherfords?'

Wickham sighed. 'They did. And the constable sent on the task was promptly told that it was the middle of the night. If they wished to speak to the grieving widow they should come back at a more appropriate hour to do so.'

'And...'

'And he did as they instructed.'

Holmes moaned in frustration.

'When he returned at breakfast time she was there.'

'Of course, she was,' Holmes lamented. 'She had the entire night in which to make the trip back, have the coach put away, have the stable boy brush down the horses, and present herself to the constable.'

Wickham replied, 'Emelia and her parents vouched for Mrs Darcy personally as having been there the entire night. No one will dare question them. They are pillars of the community. They are an old and powerful name in the area, and Mr. Rutherford owns the third largest bank in Carlisle. Would they dare put their reputation on the line for Mrs Darcy?'

Holmes offered as he poured himself another cup of coffee, 'Let us not forget that wealth blinds many a man from his conscience. I would not be surprised if in a fortnight the money she has strewn over three different banks makes its way into one—Mr Rutherford's bank. An extra two-hundred thousand pounds in the coffers might help catapult his bank into second place.'

I asked Wickham, 'Is it truly possible to get from Carlisle to Keswick and back in the span of a few hours?'

'I have done it myself several times by coach. There are two routes from here—north to Bassenthwaite then northeast to Carlisle or east to Penrith then north to Carlisle. Both are a bit over two hours one way. Even giving for inclement weather, if the horses were pushed, four hours, or probably less, could have easily gotten her here and back.'

'And we are certain it wasn't Mrs McGlinn?' I pressed.

'She began to weep openly when we told her of the news of Mr Darcy. She was completely dry, head to toe, which would have been a miracle in itself, given the state of the weather. And the only weapon she was ever known to possess was the game gun. It would have done much more damage than the small hole left in Mr Darcy's head.'

'And,' Holmes reminded me, 'we have already seen the Derringer Mrs Darcy used as protection. I have no doubt who the guilty party is. Proving it is another matter entirely. With strong support from the Rutherfords, no one will question her involvement again.'

I said, 'Quite frankly, she saved the Crown the trouble of a hanging.'

'Although I do not necessarily condone vigilantism, Watson, I agree in this case. Based on what I know, he would have hanged. And there is something to be said for a woman scorned. Mrs Darcy gave her husband everything, and it seems he gave absolutely nothing back in return. This was her remittance.'

Wickham then asked the question we both wanted answers to. 'I still cannot wrap my mind around this whole affair. How on earth did we get to this point to begin with?'

Holmes straightened himself in his seat. 'Let me see if I can shed some light on this ghastly affair for you. Now, one of the manipulators of this plot is dead and the other is currently not speaking, so I do not have the corroboration I usually have for this little summation; nonetheless, though I may be off on some little matter, of the meatier points I have no doubt.'

Wickham and I both leaned in expectantly.

Holmes raised his hand as if giving a signal to someone, and shortly Mr Bruce brought out a plate of three pickled beet eggs and set them on the table between us. 'Just as you asked, Mr Holmes. The best pickled eggs in the Lake District.'

He eyed each of us. 'Which of you would like to eat these lovely eggs?'

I replied, 'I have never been a fan of anything pickled besides herring.'

Wickham smiled. 'I have not eaten since yesterday morning. I would be more than happy to. And Mr Bruce was not kidding—these have won awards.' He picked up one of the wet, red, rubbery eggs and in two bites it was gone.

'Now, Watson, look at his fingers.'

Wickham lifted his hand and wiggled his fingers as he chewed. They were stained pink.

'Finish the other two eggs, if you would please, Mr Wickham. Mr Bruce was certain that Mr Darcy always had three.'

The man hungrily ate the other two, finally washing them down with a swill of coffee.

'Now wipe your hands as any civilized person would do upon completion of the eggs.'

Wickham did as instructed and, knowing what Holmes was going to ask next, held up again his hand for inspection. His fingers were still stained pink.

The confusion must have been obvious on my face. 'What does any of this mean?' I asked.

'Mr Darcy had pickled beet eggs as part of his lunch before he left for Workington. Even wiping one's hands afterward does not completely erase the stain they leave. Yet, when we examined Mr Darcy's body, there was no stain whatsoever on either hand. Once I had been given that information by Mrs McGlinn, I immediately began to question whether the body was, in fact, Mr Darcy at all.

'Now, let us stay with the hands for a moment,' he continued. 'They were callused from rowing, yes?'

'Correct,' Wickham interjected.

'I would like to know why he was rowing when vigorous walking through the countryside would have worked just as well, maybe even better, if weight loss was his goal?'

'I do not think we can infer anything from that,' said I incredulously. 'The type of exercise a man utilizes to lose weight is arbitrary. There are many ways of exerting one's self that can all have the desired effect of weight loss. Rowing a boat is one of them.'

'Correct, Watson, but there was a second desired effect specific to rowing that Mr Darcy was after.'

He turned to Wickham. 'Would you say that before he began his exercise regimen Mr Darcy was more—ample than Mr McGlinn?'

'By about twenty pounds easily, but he certainly was not fat.'

'And because of his occupation working aboard ships, how would you describe Mr McGlinn's hands?'

Wickham shrugged. 'I suppose they would have been rough and callused.'

Overcome with frustration from lack of sleep I asked, 'Where is all this going Holmes? Just cut to the chase and tell us.'

He smiled. 'You are impatient, Watson, when patience is needed most. What I am trying to tell you is that this was all an elaborate ruse. Mrs McGlinn and Mr Darcy had hatched a plan to kill her husband and pass him off as Mr Darcy, while they absconded with the money from the safe and left to start a new life elsewhere. Mr Darcy lost the weight, darkened in the sun, and callused his hands, so when they tried to pass off the dead Mr McGlinn, a callused and tanned deckhand, as Mr Darcy no one would be the wiser.'

'So, when did you suspect Mrs McGlinn in all of this?' Wickham asked. 'I saw nothing that would have even hinted at her involvement.'

Holmes leaned back in his chair with an air of satisfaction. 'There are few puzzles that I, having been given even a few pieces, cannot make out the picture. Here are a few more that led me to my conclusion. Mr Darcy was left handed. You, Wickham, quite off-handedly mentioned that he was the only left-handed individual in Keswick.'

'At least as far as I know,' added Wickham.

Holmes waved off the statement. 'Let us assume that he is the only left-handed individual that has a part in this drama. Based on our interactions with Mrs McGlinn and Mrs Darcy, we know they certainly are not.'

'And I can say with certainty that Mr McGlinn also was not,' Wickham added, though by the look on his face he was not sure where this was going to land.

'Now, Watson, when we were in the McGlinn home do you remember what was on the table?'

I closed my eyes and taxed my weary brain for a moment. 'I believe there was part of a loaf of bread and an open cloth of butter with a knife.'

'And their location on the table?' my friend pressed.

'I believe the bread was on the left and the butter and knife were on the right. But that is what you would expect from a right-handed individual. They held the loaf with their left hand and cut and buttered with their right.'

Holmes smiled, 'Good observation, Watson, even if incorrect. You failed to take into consideration the only chair at the table, which was on the kitchen side. Based on the placement of the knife the person was sitting in that chair when they cut and buttered the bread.'

'Which means,' said I, finishing Holmes' thought, 'that the person held the loaf in their right hand and cut and buttered with their left—they were left-handed.'

'So pickled beet eggs and left-handedness brought you to Mrs McGlinn?' Wickham asked.

A small grin creased Holmes' long face. 'I have done more with less.'

'So, Darcy was the one we chased from the house!' I exclaimed.

Wickham's brow knotted as he looked from one to the other of us. 'You gave chase? When did you see him?'

Holmes replied, 'He was trying to make an escape out the bedroom window while we and Mrs McGlinn were in the living room chatting. With his large frame, he ended up making quite the disturbance as he climbed through the opening. Although I had reason to believe it was Mr Darcy we were chasing, he disappeared into the tree line at the back of the house before we could positively identify him. There was at least a chance that it was a Gypsy attempting to pilfer food...or worse, and I reveal nothing until I am certain of all the facts I present, so I said nothing. Even now, as I sit here, I can think of another reason to believe it was not a Gypsy in that room.'

'That being...' I pressed.

'The dog never barked. Surely with its more acute hearing, it heard disturbances in the other room that we did not. Why did it not bark an alarm? It barked at us from a hundred yards away until Mrs McGlinn hushed it. The dog already knew there was someone in the house, and that person was not a stranger. It had to be someone with whom the dog was familiar, and with a nearly year-long affair, it was no doubt quite accustomed to having Mr Darcy about.' He waved his hand dismissively. 'That little clue is but a trifle to the others; however, after the failed chase, it was then that I decided to go to Workington to see if I could acquire more information on both Mr Darcy and Mr. McGlinn.'

'And what did your inquiries reveal?' I asked.

'Two important facts: One—Mr McGlinn did not find work on a ship bound for Tortola. He had been without work for several months because he had quite the temper and was always fighting with the other crew. I found many on the docks willing to speak of George McGlinn, and none of it was of an honorable sort. He had been effectively banned from working any ships out of Workington.'

Wickham nodded. 'I can attest to his short fuse. We in the village have all seen it at least once. Morwenna seemed the only one who could dampen it before it went off.'

'But Mrs McGlinn paid a price, as well,' Holmes replied.

'Yes,' I started. 'That bruise on her wrist—'

'It was not from the kitchen door at the inn closing on it, as she would have us believe. It was circumferential, not linear. It was made by someone grabbing her forcefully about the wrist'

'And what of the second fact?' Wickham asked.

'That Mr Darcy did not go to Workington as often as was thought. It seems at least half the time he travelled, he exited the train at the Braithwaite station. That was established easily enough by chatting up the ticket inspector, who often saw him getting off there instead of staying for the entire trip to the coast. I surmise that he would then traverse the four or five miles of backcountry, careful to avoid the walking trails as someone local might recognize him, to the McGlinn's to rendezvous while George McGlinn was at Workington desperately trying to find work.'

'That is why he had on his wellies and not his shoes,' I postulated. 'And that little blue flower you found in his tread—it was carpeting the hillside of the McGlinn property.'

'I knew nothing of a little blue flower,' Wickham said with just a bit of annoyance showing, which often happened when Holmes refused to reveal any of his findings until that final moment when the case has been cracked.

'It was trivial, as it turned out,' he said offhandedly. 'The countryside all around is dotted with them on the higher slopes. It only told me where he was walking but not from which direction or to where.'

Wickham pinched his nose. It was obvious the threads of the case were beginning to tangle in his mind. He said, 'Okay, so we have Morwenna and Mr Darcy having an affair. He is stepping out on his wife and sneaking to Morwenna's while George McGlinn is off looking for work, and he is supposed to be in Workington making plans for his renovations. We have established that George is a ruffian, was out of work because of it, and on at least one occasion probably gave Morwenna a bruise on her wrist, so he may have also been violent at home, as well. How do we go from that to George McGlinn getting his head lopped off? And where did the blasted sword come from?'

'The former takes a bit of postulation,' my friend replied, 'but the latter is easy. Do we all recall the suit of armour at the Darcy's?'

Wickham and I both nodded our heads in the affirmative.

'It had its hand raised as if in battle, yet it was empty of any implement of war. At some point, Darcy extricated it from the home unseen. In all probability, Mrs Darcy was too busy giving the home her womanly touch to have noticed a missing piece of old armour. Watson, I certainly thought that would not have passed your gaze.'

'Sorry to disappoint,' I replied unfazed as I poured myself more coffee. 'If I were to catch every minutia put before me, there would be no use for you, then, now would there?'

Wickham chuckled at the cheeky remark.

Even Holmes smiled. 'Touché, Watson. Now, postulating the former, let me see if I can sum it up thusly: During their months-long affair, no doubt Mrs McGlinn inquired about the key around Mr Darcy's neck, having ample opportunity to see it unencumbered by clothing. Maybe he was hesitant at first to divulge its secret. Maybe he revealed it straightaway. At some point, probably when she revealed she was carrying his child, they schemed the plan to steal the money from his safe. But they had to be able to leave without the fear of being found out. They wanted anonymity, not to spend the rest of their lives on the run from authorities. They would kill her husband and pass him off as Mr Darcy. Darcy would then steal the money from the safe. Whomever the thief might be, no one would suspect someone already dead. Mrs McGlinn started circulating the lie that her husband had found work and would be gone for months. She would stay on in Keswick for a few more weeks, then leave just as she said she would. The two would meet up somewhere, probably Penrith where Mr Darcy was less known, then take a train to their new life, which was more than likely nowhere near Cornwall. That was their plan as I see it.'

'How did you know where to find the sword and the head?' Wickham asked.

'The henhouse was the most logical place to hide them with quick work yet needing done. They still had to clean the area of blood as best they could, switch clothing, and get the body to the road to be found the next day. Hidden in a pile of hay among the chickens was the perfect place. Besides, no one would suspect her. By the time any new tenants found the evidence, she and Mr Darcy would have effectively disappeared. It is even possible, dare I say *likely,* that the henhouse was only a temporary repository of the head and the implement of its severance. Surely, there were better, more remote places all around the countryside in which to permanently hide them when the time was right.' He then nodded in Wickham's direction and emphasized. 'Even, might I add, the bottom of Derwentwater.'

'Do you think that is where the murder happened?' I asked. 'In the enclosure with the chickens?'

'No. I believe it happened at the side porch where we first saw her hanging laundry. Mrs McGlinn was more than likely on the porch and her husband in the grass at the bottom of the stairs facing her. She led him to the side porch on one pretense or another. They would have been nearly eye to eye. She had him engaged, possibly in a purposely instigated argument, while Darcy crept up from behind from around the chicken enclosure, sword drawn for the fatal blow. I saw some discoloration to the grass, which she endeavored to cover with her laundry basket. When we were attempting to finally convince her to come to town after giving chase to whom we now know was Mr Darcy, she must have intimated my seeing the stain for she kicked the basket, feigning frustration, which then covered the rest of the stain. I did not let on that I had noticed anything, as I did not want to show my hand early for there were other questions still needing to be answered. Unfortunately, there will probably be very little of that evidence left after last night's rain.'

Wickham said, 'I shall relay that information to Dunne. It may be that she will be more likely to admit to it if we can prove to her we already know the details.'

'Possibly,' said Holmes. 'It may also be that we shall be party to a sensational trial in the coming months in which I would be more than happy to lend my testimony.'

'Then there is Mrs Darcy,' I said. 'What of her and her part in the actual killing of Mr Darcy?'

'I shall leave that to the Carlisle Constabulary and Chief Constable Dunne, as he seems unlikely to employ my services. I suspect, Watson, that she will not be charged if even investigated further in his death. Her alibi is incontrovertible so long as the Rutherfords are willing to stand by her.' He shrugged lazily. 'For some reason, I do not feel the urge to push the issue. Darcy would have faced the gallows, of that I am certain. The executioner is never incriminated in the death of his charge, so who am I to question the identity of the executioner?'

I said, 'I am still at a loss as to why she even returned.'

'Anger is often amalgamated with sorrow at the death of a loved one,' Holmes replied. 'And Mrs Darcy's anger had begun to overtake her in due course. She showed as much when she admitted to wanting—no, hoping—to use her Derringer on the intruder that first night. I am sure it was a fright looking in on him through the billiard room window. At the hearing of the depth and scope of his betrayal, no doubt that anger turned to rage, and in that state, she was capable of transgressions of the highest order.'

At last, likely feeling that all the questions that could be answered now were, Wickham stood and yawned. 'I am just glad this whole affair is for the most part finished. Maybe Keswick can get back to some normalcy once again. And just in time, too. In a few weeks we shall be overrun with religious fervor as a yearly convention comes to town. Poor Keswick could use some prayers.'

'As could we all, Mr. Wickham,' replied Holmes.

We spent one more day in Keswick. I slept, and Holmes sat at his room's window and smoked his shag tobacco while watching it rain on Skiddaw off in the distance.

. . . . .

As an epilogue to this little affair, there are two things of note. The first is that the sensational trial Holmes had spoken of never materialised. Morwenna McGlinn finally broke her silence, once Wickham relayed what Holmes had told him. She admitted to her involvement in the plan to kill her husband, but it was, in fact, Mr Darcy who struck the fatal blow. She vehemently denied having anything whatever to do with the actual killing of Mr Darcy, which we had already surmised. She was charged with both, nonetheless, although no one could adequately explain how she killed Mr Darcy. She pleaded for mercy and gave abuse at the hands of her husband as extenuating circumstances. It was not given. Her baby was taken from her after weaning, and a year to the day that we stepped off the train in Keswick Mrs Morwenna McGlinn was hanged at Carlisle.

The second is that Holmes was correct in his assumption on Mrs Darcy's money. Within a month she had terminated two of her bank accounts and put her entire fortune in Rutherford's bank at Carlisle. She stayed with the family until one week after Mrs McGlinn's hanging. She then boarded a steamer back to Boston, where coincidentally, the Rutherfords conveniently have a bank branch. She was never seen on this Isle again, as far as can be ascertained by occasional queries by Holmes. To this day the Rutherfords have never changed their story, and to this day Holmes believes Mrs Darcy killed her husband.

This sad story is not yet finished, as far as the town itself is concerned. There is one more trifle that needs mentioning before I rest my pen. It was August 15th, three weeks after returning to Baker Street that I found myself perusing the Morning Post, and Holmes was finally reading the book I had given him while on holiday. Not looking for anything in particular to read but merely skimming the pages, my eyes came across a familiar name, and I read the headline out loud, 'The Derwentwater Disaster.'

Holmes stopped reading and looked at me expectantly. It is possible he thought the article some little piece regarding the Darcy affair in Keswick. I admit to the same sentiments before I read the article.

I read through the first few paragraphs of the article silently then cleared my throat and summed it up, 'It seems that on the twelfth of August five young women from a religious convention and two men were out on the lake when a sudden storm whipped up. The boat capsized in the tumultuous waves. The five women were lost, and two men survived.' I put the paper down and sighed, remembering what Constable Wickham had said to us that last morning. I said, 'So much for the prayers for poor Keswick.'

Holmes closed the book, stood and picked up his clay pipe from the mantel. He was quiet at first, as he filled it with tobacco. Finally, he said in a sombre tone, 'It is bad enough, Watson, that we expend so much grey matter concocting ways in which to exterminate each other.' He lit it and took a long inhalation. The smoke left him in a long sigh. 'We tend to forget there are times when even Mother Nature seems to have no need of us.'

The End

Author's thoughts

Even though the story is fiction, the town of Keswick in the Lake District and The Derwentwater Disaster briefly alluded to at the end are real. It was the purest of happenstance that my story took place a few weeks before the real tragedy. On August 12th, 1898, five young ladies were drowned in a boating accident on Derwentwater in Keswick. My friend Ray Greenhow, who I mentioned in my acknowledgments, researched and wrote their long-forgotten story in the book titled The Derwentwater Disaster: 12 August, 1898. It can be bought at www.bookscumbria.com.

I hoped you liked the story. If you did, I also have two other Sherlock Holmes stories out. The Mystery of the Broken Window, and A Reflection of Evil. They can be found here:

https://www.amazon.com/Sherlock-Holmes-Mystery-Broken-Window-ebook/dp/B01N1KXITP

https://www.amazon.com/Reflection-Evil-Sherlock-Holmes-Mystery-ebook/dp/B06XKYK5LV

Both are also out in audiobook on Audible.com and Amazon. The following pages have excerpts from both books. Enjoy.

The Mystery of the Broken Window

1

As Sherlock Holmes, in a persistently argumentative mood as of late, has gone to visit—and more than likely annoy—his brother Mycroft, I sit here in blissful yet rare silence, pouring over the volumes of cases, some of which may never see the light of day. I revel in the sheer accomplishment of my dear friend. In the years since we first took up residence here at Baker Street, innumerable characters have pleaded their cases in this very room. All piqued Holmes's intellect to one extent or another. They were his test tubes in the chemistry set of life. None, it seems to me, could elicit from his stalwart countenance anything akin to empathy. That is not to say that he did not care for the well-being of these people. On several occasions, when either his services were summoned too late or clues were not presenting themselves in a timely manner and tragedy ensued—such as that curious case of The

Five Orange Pips—Holmes became even more tenacious in his duty to place the guilty parties in the dock. His compassion was shown through the application of his unique abilities that brought about justice that oft times slipped through more authoritative hands.

But there was one case that I feel, as his raconteur, shows a more human side to that genius of deduction and logic. There have only been a handful of events during the years we have spent together that elicited emotions that Holmes often said were detestable to the machinations of a mind such as his. But it warmed me immensely to be a part of those occasions, for they steeled my fondness of the man. In this particular account, it was brought out, albeit briefly, by a golden-haired fifteen-year-old girl, whose name was Fiona Hopkins.

It was during the summer of '84, a Tuesday afternoon, the sixteenth of July. Each of us was engrossed in our own separate tasks, he at his beakers and Bunsen burners and I at wallowing through the trudge that is London news. A cooling breeze was wafting the curtains of the open window, letting in the hustle and bustle from Baker Street below.

'I fancy we shall be receiving company shortly,' said Holmes never looking up from his experiment.

'Now how on earth can you know that?' I asked as I pulled the paper from my line of sight.

He nodded to the open window.

'And what do you make of all that dissonance?' I asked, my curiosity piqued.

'Come now, Watson. Do you not hear the hansom on the street below?'

'I hear several. How do you know any of them are for us?'

He stretched his lean neck, bending his ear slightly closer to the window. 'It is no different scrutinizing evidence to see which is relevant and which is happenstance. The cacophony below is the evidence to our ear. We must discard that which isn't needed and decipher that which is left. Do you not hear the slowing of the hooves, the increase in its timbre, as it nears and halts below?'

'I will take you at your word, but what makes you think that particular hansom has us in mind?'

Just as he was about to offer up an explanation, there was a ring at the bell downstairs.

Holmes smirked, and I for my turn just shook my head in amazement.

'My powers of supposition are rather strong, my dear Watson. Without it, an investigation will never get off the ground. With it, you have as equal a chance at being wrong as you do right. I usually like my odds.'

Just then, Mrs Hudson hurried in a young man no older than twenty.

A Reflection of Evil

Chapter 1

While the year 1896 was not a particularly eventful year regarding cases in which to showcase my friend Sherlock Holmes' remarkable abilities, it was a sombrely dynamic year, nonetheless. In the ten months or so between the particulars surrounding the Bruce Partington Plans in November of '95 through the mystery Holmes cleared up in the Veiled Lodger in September of '96, very little took place in the life of the restless boarders of 221B Baker Street. The monumental volume of crimes typical in a city of this size, especially those of which Holmes was especially astute in solving, seemed to have been chiseled down to bric-a-brac of the sort that Holmes would never stoop to waste his intellect on.

Things looked bleak. That is until a Mrs Anne Merrick walked into our digs.

It was the 26th of June 1896, a warm and breezy Friday. Sherlock Holmes was staring languidly at the wall, chewing on his spent pipe, while I scoured the papers for any trifle worth mentioning to him.

'It seems a Mr and Mrs Templeton in Poplar have somehow misplaced a few of their Schipperkes,' I said aloud to bring Holmes out of his melancholy.

'Excuse me?' he replied dryly.

'Schipperkes—they are dogs. The Templetons are breeders.'

He sighed and turned a twisted brow to me. 'I know what Schipperkes are, Watson.'

'Well, what do you think?' I asked.

'About what?'

'Finding them. They are offering a fairly sizable reward. Several dogs are missing.'

Holmes turned defiantly, taking the pipe from his mouth. 'Watson, do you honestly think I would waste my time trapesing the countryside looking for what amounts to be a pack of primped and pampered black rats? The fact that they are offering a reward is inconsequential. I need stimuli, not compensation.'

Putting the paper down I faced him directly. 'Wouldn't that be better than just wasting our afternoon caged in this den of filth and smoke you have created. If nothing else, it will get us outside into the fresh air.'

Holmes said nothing, which relayed to me his utter disinterest. He only straightened his lean frame from the chair and retrieved a box next to the mantel. This the detective placed on his lap when reseated and began pulling out locks of different shapes and sizes. Once a lock was within his grasp, he tinkered with the locking mechanisms of each with a personally-fashioned tool he had retrieved from the stand next to his chair. Within several seconds of manipulating the small tool inside each lock, they would pop open and he would toss it over his shoulder, ending in a loud thud upon the wooden floor at his back. He then repeated this same action with each subsequent lock. Within ten minutes, fifteen open locks lay haphazardly along the floor behind the man.

I was about to remonstrate him on the metallic minefield he had created across our flooring when there came a knock at the door.

'Yes, Mrs Hudson?' said Sherlock Holmes as he put his little tool in the pocket of his frock coat.

Mrs Hudson entered the room with a tall, young lady in tow. 'A Mrs Anne Merrick with some urgent business. And may I say, whatever it is she needs your assistance with, please take it. The confounded noises and awful smells coming from this room will be the death of me.'

Ignoring Mrs Hudson's remark, Holmes rose and, regarding the young lady, gestured to his seat. 'Please, sit here and tell me what has brought you to our humble abode.'

Made in the USA
Middletown, DE
04 November 2018